TURBULENCE

Ross Richdale

2022

This is a work of fiction. Similarities to real people, places, or events are entirely coincidental.

TURBULENCE

First edition. March 16, 2022.

ISBN: 978-1877438882

Written by Ross Richdale.

Turbulence

Ross Richdale

Ellie Parkes and Wyatt Sigley meet during a ferocious storm when he rescues her from the surf at the remote Greystone Beach on the southeastern coast of New Zealand's North Island. Due to a collapsed bridge over a flooded river that also wrecks her car, Ellie agrees to stay at Wyatt's homestead until she can get out. There she tells him a little about her school life and home problems.

Both of them find they come from dysfunctional marriages with Wyatt defending his divorced wife, Jennifer's claim for half the value of the homestead that had been in his family for several generations. Ellie is a victim of a dominating husband, Jaxon with the ongoing violence who resents her successful position as a school principal at Thomas Road School.

After returning to town and with Wyatt's help, Ellie shifts out to an apartment in the centre of Hutt City, her hometown. Jaxon attempts to find her and mistakenly thinks an apartment in a newly built apartment block is where she lives. Annette Patterson, a lawyer lives there. When a bomb is detonated in the building she survives but is hospitalised with burns.

Ellie meets and invites Annette to share her apartment until she can move back to another rebuilt one. They become friends and one weekend Annette accepts an invitation to accompany Ellie and Wyatt to his homestead.

Nearby, trampers Scarlett, Nolan and Karson become involved in a conflict with Jaxon at McArthur's Hut in the forest park. Later they meet up with Ellie and Wyatt at the homestead and tell them that he is in the district.

They see Jaxon watching and decide to leave using Wyatt's utility vehicle to take a track through to Riversdale Beach, the closest settlement to their north. Jaxon sets fire to the homestead but later discovers they had left and were not trapped inside as he had planned. He follows them on his motorbike hell bend on shooting them on sight.

Will the increasingly schizophrenic Jaxon succeed in his murderous quest to assassinate them all or do they, with the help of local police manage to escape his clutches?

All will be told in this romantic thriller as Ellie and Wyatt's two lives become intertwined and friendliness and appreciation turns to love.

CHAPTER 1

The storm in mid-year 2017 was the worst of the winter. Three metre high tidal waves pounded Greystone Beach on the southeastern coast of Wairarapa, a district in New Zealand's North Island. Spray and the occasional actual wave hit the country road before retreating with debris splattered everywhere.

A Toyota Land Cruiser swerved around a gigantic tree trunk that remained across half the road and proceeded on at a snail's pace. Inside, the driver flicked off the button to his plugged-in iPhone for the signal had disappeared. It always cut out further back along the road when a nearby hill blocked the signal. Locals were considering building their own repeater up the hill behind his property but couldn't agree on how it would be paid for. Perhaps he should just go ahead and pay for a smaller version on the rise behind the homestead himself.

He thought back to a few moments earlier when the call cut out. It was only Jennifer, his ex-wife. He had thought the settlement after their divorce was more than fair but now she was after the half share of the homestead. After the death of his parents this was now his and he'd be damned if Jennifer would get her greedy claws into it.

The next wave crashed on the beach but was not as bad as the earlier ones. High tide would have been reached by now. These spring tides were always a problem but this year they appeared worse than usual.

The road ahead rose on the inland side of a rocky outcrop and followed a two kilometre beach and tiny beach settlement before turning back into the hills and the homestead. Spray from the breaking waves forced him to increase the windscreen wiper speed as he peered ahead. Once on the straight section that followed the beach he increased speed a little. He enjoyed the moods of the Pacific Ocean from being mirror-like in the summer through to today's winter July storm.

As another huge wave formed off shore, he blinked and wiped his eyes. A woman was standing in shallow surf that swirled around her legs. She wore a raincoat, jeans and blonde hair blew in the wind.

"Stupid womanl," he muttered.

He braked to a stop and tooted the horn but was ignored.

That wave building out beyond her was huge and close to shore. It curled like those massive waves in Hawaii that surfers rode but with one difference; it shuddered in the wind and broke as it cut across retreating foam. At the same time another wave thundered across from the south,

This was treacherous and no place for the spectator to be standing.

The breaking main wave was hit by this rogue side one that also broke, surf rose high in the air before crashing back in a choppy swirl. When the broken waves headed towards the beach he stared out. The woman had disappeared!

"Oh hell!" he gasped. "Come on, Cinders."

He braked, jumped out of the Land Cruiser and tore along the wet sand, closely followed by his Black Labrador dog. Everywhere was crashing surf but he thought he saw arms stretched up beyond the next mounting wave.

He hauled off his work boots and jacket and tossed them beyond the water's edge. Now in his old shirt and shorts that he always wore when visiting the homestead, he plunged into the surf twenty metres or so north of the woman. Cinders followed along through the surf barking.

His knowledge of local conditions was perfect! He dropped beneath the mountain of water about to break, came out the far side and allowed the waves to carry him towards her. There she was thrashing frantically in another gap between the breakers. If he didn't reach her before the next wave broke there was no way to predict where she could end up!

She disappeared!

But no, there she was thrashing in the waves further out,

He swam with all his might and just before the next breaker broke, grabbed her from behind.

She struggled, turned and flung arms around his neck almost choking him as they were sucked beneath the wave in a green coloured swirl.

He held the woman but her weight hindered his effort to get to the surface. He kicked out, ignored her legs that thumped into him and managed to continue to hold her. Shining light showed above! They broke surface, he gasped for breath and was sucked under again still with her held firmly against him.

Time appeared to stop as he struggled to reach the surface again. He managed to do so just as another wave broke overhead. This one headed straight in carrying them both with it. He was flipped over and scrapped his legs on sand. Hell, that hurt!

He found he could touch sand and stood up. The woman began coughing and spluttering but also stood just as more surf surrounded them. They headed for shore and managed to crawl forward before retreating water sucked them back out.

He let the woman go and like her, found himself spluttering and spitting out salty water.

"Come on, we need to get up the beach," he said. "Another wave is coming!"

She turned and stared at him for the first time. "Thank you. It all just happened!" Her lips quivered and she would have fallen if he didn't reach out and steady her.

"It's okay," he said. "You're safe now. My Land Cruiser is up on the road and we're only a kilometre from my place. He held out a hand. "Name's Wyatt Sigley and this is my dog Cinders."

He nodded at a very wet Black Labrador who sat gazing at the woman with his tail wagging.

She shivered and gave a slight smile as she stepped back. "Ellie Parkes," she said in a soft voice. "Thank you again, Wyatt."

She gave the dog a pat.

Wyatt nodded and they both headed up a sand bank away from another line of chasing foam.

When they reached the Land Cruiser he grabbed a towel from the back seat and grinned at her after she accepted it and climbed in the front passenger seat.

"Be back in tick," he said. "Need to get my boots and jacket off the beach. Have you anything lying around?"

She shook her head.

He returned a moment later and climbed into the driver's seat. "So how did you get here?" he asked.

"Car ran out of gas about a kilometre back. I was heading for Riversdale."

Wyatt grimaced. "You were lost. It's about twenty kilometres north of here but there is no coastal road. You need to go all the way back to the main highway, north to Masterton and take a different route to the coast."

"When I hit the narrow gravel road I assumed that and had actually turned around and was heading back when my car spluttered and stopped. Stupid woman!"

"Well, we'll get you home and into dry clothes. I can get a can of gas and we'll then go back to your car. "

"Dry clothes? Is your partner there?"

"My ex," Wyatt replied. "She was about your size and some of her clothes are still there."

"And she won't mind?"

Wyatt shrugged. "Who cares?" he almost snorted but caught Ellie's eyes. "Sorry, we had a bad break up. I haven't actually seen her for a couple of years."

"Sorry."

"Don't be. It was inevitable and for the best."

She just looked away and pouted. "Thank you. Dry clothes would be appreciated and the petrol too, of course."

"That's fine," Wyatt replied and started the Land Cruiser.

WHEN THEY DROVE INTO his home driveway, Ellie looked at the elegant two storey house of a bygone era.

"What a grand old building," she said. "Are you a local farmer?"

Wyatt grinned. "No, I'm an real estate agent from Wellington."

"Sigley's Real Estate?"

That's the one. I started out ony own a couple of years ago. We recently opened a branch in Hitt City." Wyatt grinned and changed the topic, "This is the original homestead of South Pacific View Station. The farm had been in our family for four generations. but was sold off by my grandmother twenty years back. However, for sentimental reasons she kept the house and twenty acres of land in the family's name. After my parents died I inherited it."

"So you don't live here permanently?"

Wyatt shook his head. "I try to get here on a regular basis. My few acres around are leased to the owners of our original farm, an overseas conglomerate. I've been renovating this building more or less as a hobby." He grinned. "It has a Category 2 restriction by the government Historic Places Trust placed on it."

Ellie glanced at him. "Meaning?"

"Basically, it cannot be pulled down or have any external features altered. I can do whatever I like inside that doesn't affect the external appearance." He pointed up. "See that chimney?"

She nodded.

"It leads nowhere inside but had to be strengthened from the inside so the outside appearance remained the same. About a decade back, I remember my father mumbling about the cost and that it would have been far easier to just pull it down."

"So now it's an earthquake risk?"

Wyatt laughed. "Probably. I think the new earthquake regulations and those for historic buildings are are in conflict with each other."

ELLIE GLANCED AROUND the upstairs bedroom where Wyatt had left her to select some of his previous wife's clothes to wear. The room appeared clean and tidy but had that musty aroma of being unused. She was hesitant about completely changing but selected a cotton blouse and pair of jeans to try on and walked along to an older type bathroom to rinse off salty water from herself.

She shivered and turned to where an old fashioned three-quarter sized mirror reflected her body. Her arms were covered in old bruises not caused by her time in the water and there were the latest purple ones where her husband, Jaxon had hit her in the stomach. The bastard never hit her where it showed but lately as his violence became more severe he had become less fussy.

The stranger's dry clothes were a little bulky but not too bad and far better than her previous clinging ones. She shivered, perhaps from the cold and added a loose fitting jacket that would cover her arms. Realising she had no shoes she found some flat heeled ones that were also a little large but not too bad.

She found a clean looking hairbrush to use and headed back downstairs and along a corridor to the kitchen where the smell of coffee filled the air.

Wyatt had also changed and grinned at her when she walked in. "I don't think your car will be going anywhere so how about a coffee and a bite to eat before we head back to get it?" He glanced at the wet clothes she was carrying. "We can put those through a wash or I can get a plastic bag for them."

"Thanks," Ellie said. "I'd like them to be washed and the idea of coffee and food is appreciated."

For a moment there was silence as she sat on a breakfast nook stool and watched him remove some buns from a microwave and pour steaming water from a kettle into two mugs.

He slid one along the bench to her and nodded at a container of milk and some satchels standing in a jar. "Only instant coffee I'm afraid. Help yourself to milk and sweetener. Margarine on your bun?"

"Thanks." Ellie smiled as she reached for the milk. "Instant coffee is fine and I prefer margarine to butter and sweetener rather than sugar."

"Local dairy farmers would think we're traitors but one must move with the times."

"'Indeed so," Ellie whispered and felt glad she had not been offered a beer or wine. She hated the stuff! Jaxon's leering face and taunts flicked across her mind and in some ways this was worse that her conservative parents views on that subject. Moving from one extreme to another hadn't been easy.

"You're deep in thought," Wyatt said. "I'm sure your car will be fine. I doubt if there'll be any visitors around and locals will think it's just parked while someone went for a bush or beach walk. There's a bush hut in the hills about a couple of hours walking distance away. It's amazing how visitors just park and wander around." He stood up. "I'll get that can of gas while you finish off your coffee. At least there appears to be a lull in the storm but the weather forecast predicts more thunder showers"

THE RAIN HAD STOPPED but clouds out to sea looked ominous as Wyatt drove back along the road with Ellie beside him and Cinders on the back seat. To their right the waves still thundered in but high tide had been reached so surf did not reach the road. Mind you, debris including tree trunks were strewn everywhere.

"I guess I walked a couple of kilometres," Ellie said. "I managed to get my car off the road in what looked like a passing bay near the river.

"I think I know the place," Wyatt said as he slowed to avoid another tree trunk slung across half the road.

THEY HAD TRAVELLED less than a kilometre away from the coast when Wyatt drove around a bend and swore as he slammed on the brakes. Ahead, the normal small river was a raging current of swirling brown flood waters. Worse though was that the bridge, normally a one way structure often found on local country roads had gone. All that remained were two supporting beams with tree trunks and other debris piled up behind and half the broken decking that sloped down into the water. The rest was caught under some overhanging trees about twenty metres downstream.

"The district council should have replaced the bridge years ago," he muttered.

Ellie just stared at the scene and pointed towards the trees "Oh my God?' she asked. "Look!"

Wyatt followed her gaze. There amongst the decking and tree trunks he made out four wheels sticking up and a glimpse of red paint. A car had been tossed over and lay partly submerged amongst the debris.

"Your car?" He asked the obvious.

Ellie just nodded."Why did I have to park by the river?" she finally whispered.

Wyatt reached across and gave her arm a gentle squeeze. "You weren't to know and anyway if you'd run out of gas you couldn't have gone any further."

"Guess not," Ellie said. "All my gear and laptop are in the car."

"But you weren't. Things can be replaced."

Ellie nodded. "You're right! I can cancel my holiday rental at Riversdale so if you can get me to Masterton via an alternative route I'll take a train home."

Wyatt knew that the railway commuter service between Masterton and Wellington, New Zealand's capital city, ran through Hutt City where Ellie she she lived. He grimaced. "I'm afraid that's not possible. These are all dead end roads to these remote beaches. There is no alternative route. So it's back to my place, I'm afraid."

Ellie took her mobile out of a pocket and pouted. "No signal."

"Yeah I know. It comes in at the top of the next hill on the other side of the river." He nodded through the misty rain that had begun falling again as he reversed, found a place to turn and headed back.

"If you don't mind being with a stranger you can stay with me. Otherwise I do hold a key to a couple of beach cottages at the beach. I keep an eye on them for the owners and they said I could use them any time."

Ellie shook her head. "Your place will be fine. Aren't strangers just friends you haven't met?" she asked.

Wyatt laughed and caught her eyes. "I guess so but we have met, haven't we?"

THE DREAM WAS TERRIFYING and probably a re-enactment of Ellie's thoughts about what really happened. She awoke to find she had kicked the blankets off her bed and it was freezing. It took a few seconds to stare around the blackened room, not that she could see much. In fact she could see nothing, not even the reflection through the top window from streetlights because there were none!

And why was she asleep in bulky day clothes?

It all came back as she pulled blankets up around herself but was no light switch within reach. She lay there with her heart thumping. She was in an upstairs bedroom in Wyatt's ancestral home and everything was fine. Jaxon wasn't there with his leering voice and the last violent attack that she swore would be the last.

She was safe but was she?

Her eyes became adjusted to the darkness and she could now see a faint outline of the door. Someone or something moved!

Oh my God! Wyatt seemed such a nice guy but she didn't really know him!

"Who is it?" She tried to calm her trembling voice.

The reply made her concerns evaporate and relief flooded her veins when a faint whimper hit her ears.

"Cinders!" she almost sobbed. "Did you hear me cry out in my sleep?"

There was a tiny yelp and the Labrador leaped up on the double bed and gave her cheek a tiny lick as if to say that everything was okay. He would help her!

"Oh Cinders,'" she said as she reached out and hugged him. She loved dogs but they were usually smaller breeds that her family had when she grew up.

Cinders sat back across the bed with his tail wagging so fast it hit her arm. He stretched out, and seemed to be contented to be just a friend.

Ellie lay back and tried to replace the thoughts of the attack with more pleasant ones as she dropped back to sleep and into another dream. This time she was in the ocean and just about drowning. Just as she was about to sink beneath down in the waves she jerked awake.

Now though, it was dawn and almost seven on that winter day. Sound asleep across the bed was Cinders, still with his tail faintly wagging.

IT WAS AFTER EIGHT before Ellie awoke again and found Cinders gone. She had a shower and redressed in her own clothes. They were dry but slightly crumpled, not that she cared. She grinned at the thought of her, oh so precise deputy principal at Thomas Road School seeing her now. Janice Prindle was about her own age but could almost be classified as an old maid with her prim and proper outlook on life. Mind you, she was not antagonistic, as Ellie had been led to expect after her own appointment as principal. She found out later that Janice had also applied for the position that she had won. Though formal, Janice was an excellent teacher of the senior syndicate and was beginning to become a friend even when away from the school environment.

As Ellie walked down the stairs Cinders rushed up to greet her. She gave him a rub between ears. The smell of coffee and cooking bacon filled the air. She walked in and noticed Wyatt in front of the stove turning some sizzling eggs in a frying pan over.

He glanced up and grinned. "I hope you like a good old country breakfast," he said.

'Wonderful," she replied and pulled up a stool behind the quite modern kitchen sink.

"And was Cinders a pain?" Wyatt said after handing her plate of delicious looking food.

"Not at all. In fact he was exactly the opposite."

"We heard you cry out and she was off straight away," he said. "So you relived the time in the waves?" He grimaced. "'It can happen. I woke up in a hot sweat, too."

"No it was something else."

"Your husband?"

She nodded.

"It's okay," he said. "But say no more. I don't want to interfere."

"You aren't. Like Cinders, you have been so helpful. Several times, actually. Now, this wonderful breakfast..." She stopped eating and smiled at him. "Sorry to be such a hindrance."

"Anything but," Wyatt whispered and glanced away, almost as if he was embarrassed.

Ellie glanced around at the relaxing scene and her mind drifted back over everything that had happened recently.

CHAPTER 2

It had been a bad week at school with the home situation compounded by the pressures of work. By Thursday a conflict between her DP, Janice Prindle and one of the teachers in her syndicate, Kerenza Bardell had reached a climax. Both were headstrong women but a generation apart in their attitudes. They both came to her at different times during the week to complain about the other.

Kerenza taught a Year 5 class of ten-year-old children and ran a relaxed if somewhat noisy classroom. She was conscientious and spent hours of out-of-school time preparing work and enhancing her classroom with children's work. Her interest in art showed through with numerous large murals on various topics displayed on her classroom walls. In Ellie's opinion, she was one of the best teachers on the staff.

Janice, in contrast expected her syndicate teachers of the Year 5 and 6 to conform to her ideals. Kerenza in a tearful meeting with Ellie said she was doing everything asked of her. In the other meeting Janice stated that she wasn't, Kerenza's class was too noisy and programs the syndicate had agreed to follow were being brushed aside for, in her words, arty murals that wasted time.

This had been happening since not long after Kerenza's appointment a year earlier but had become worse lately. It had to stop!

She called a meeting with the pair after school that day and did the rumours fly around the school with really two camps that supported one or the other. Unusually, Ellie held the meeting in her office and even more unusual, she sat behind her desk in a formal approach.

Both her subordinates knew she was annoyed. Janice sat down stony-faced while Kerenza just stared out an office window.

"You know I am not the autocratic principal that you have both probably encountered when you went to school but this impasse between the pair of you cannot and will not continue. Neither of you are entirely at fault nor, I might add, completely blameless," Ellie began in a stern tone.

She stopped and fixed her eyes on them both alternatively for several seconds before continuing. "There is a long term solution that will be brought in later in the year and an immediate one of that will be imposed straight away."

"And they are?" Janice whispered.

"Firstly, the long term solution. The school has three syndicates with you, Janice in charge of the senior Year 5 and 6s as well as your deputy principal duties. The middle and junior syndicates each have a senior staff member in charge."

"We know that," Janice almost spat.

Ellie glowered at her and held a hand and finger up slightly.

"From the beginning of Term 4, the juniors shall remain the same. However for Year 3 to 6 children, there will be two parallel syndicates." She glared at Janice. "You'll have one, Janice and Diane our middle syndicate leader, the other." She switched her eyes to Kerenza. "You are an excellent teacher of our older children, Kerenza. When the change takes place, you will keep a Year 5 class but be placed in Diane's syndicate."

Janice almost stood up. "You can't do this," she spat.

"I can and will," Ellie retorted. "Sit down!"

Janice did.

"But what now?" Kerenza whispered. "Term four is several months away."

"This has been more difficult but after confidential discussions with our Board of Trustees a solution they actually suggested will be immediately acted upon."

Kerenza paled and her hand shook as she stared at Ellie. Janice starred at her too and there was a slight quiver in her lips as she waited.

Ellie switched her eyes to her junior teacher. "Your classroom and indeed your present class will remain the same, Kerenza. However, I am removing it from Janice's syndicate and until the new organisation takes place you will answer directly to myself." She switched her eyes back to Janice. "Your syndicate will drop from five classroom teachers to four. This will in no way affect your salary or DP duties that will not be altered. Kerenza will remain like any other teacher from the two other syndicates and be subject to your designated authority as deputy principal." She stood up, placed her hands flat on her desk and again stared at them both. "My actions are fully endorsed by our Board of Trustees and start from this moment. Understand!"

Janice just nodded while Kerenza burst into tears. "I thought you were going to sack me," she cried. "Thank you."

"I couldn't do that even if I wanted to, which I didn't," Ellie replied. "We will meet as the syndicates do every second week to discuss your class progress, planning and so forth. Think of it as being another syndicate; not just allowing you to do whatever you wish."

"I understand," Kerenza wiped her eyes with a tissue and smiled for the first time. "I shall do my upmost to support you and the school." She turned to Janice and held out her hand. "We are still colleagues, Janice and I apologise for our clash of personalities."

Janice muttered a short but positive reply before she turned to Ellie and extended her hand. Ellie shook it, grateful that her DP had accepted everything professionally.

LATELY THURSDAY WAS always a difficult time at home for Ellie. This was Jaxon's so called night out with the boys that she knew was an excuse when he became involved in casual affairs with women. Afterwards she could always tell by his attitude that ranged from being moody if things had gone wrong to being on a high if he had drunk too much.

Mainly because her position as principal had occupied most of her time she had tolerated Jaxon when his behaviour became worse over the last few months. Then, the violence had begun. He was a strong man and any attempts to fight back merely aggravated the situation. Recently trying to calm him down with rational talk failed.

She concluded that their marriage was a sham and a separation was the only way to continue her life. However, she had procrastinated on the slim hope, she guessed, that he would improved as he accepted that on the income side she was now the main money earner in the family. Also, their earlier hopes of having a family would never eventuate.

As usual, Jaxon blamed her for this but after she had taken tests her doctor stated that there was no reason that she couldn't have children. Jaxon had flatly refused to have tests and confessed at one stage that he never wanted a family anyway. This was really the beginning of the downward spiral of their relationship.

Ellie sighed as she heard his car come drive in and heard the car door slam. She embraced herself for another argument or a sullen silence. At least, when he was in one of his silent moods, violence never followed.

"Why is my meal cold?" he muttered to break his silent mood after his arrival.

"It was ready when you usually get home" Ellie retorted. "Put it in the microwave for a couple of minutes." She swallowed and stared at him. 'This cannot go on. I have decided to take the weekend away and consider my options."

"Where?" he muttered after he placed his food in the microwave.

"I've taken up an offer from one our parents to stay at their cottage at Riversdale Beach over the weekend. "

"And you never even bothered to ask me?" Jaxon hissed.

"Why should I?" Ellie retorted. "When have you ever asked me when you decide to have a weekend away on a hunting trip with your buddies?"

For a moment Jaxon almost looked calm. "That's different. You know I like hunting."

"Oh your usual double standard is it?" Ellie was annoyed and momentarily forgot to keep a calm approach.

"Bitch!' Jaxon howled, stood up and flung his chair aside.

He stepped forward, grabbed her arm and plunged his fist into her stomach.

She was winded as she doubled over in excruciating pain and staggered backwards. She reached out and just managed to steady herself by grabbing the table before sinking to her knees. Her stomach heaved.

But more was to come!

A boot kicked her in the ribs as she attempted to move away. He hauled her to her feet by her hair and he stared into her eyes.

"So the almighty school principal who can demote her DP and fire a junior teacher, isn't so bossy now, is she?" he sneered.

She was slapped across the face but worse was the second punch into her stomach that again sent her sprawling across the room. Chairs went flying and she hit something that sliced through her upper arm. In a haze of semi-consciousness she saw a blood stained smashed plate before her.

The attack continued until she managed to crawl behind the breakfast nook and pull herself up. She reached out, grabbed a pot and flung it around in a seemly futile attempt to ward Jaxon off.

The pot hit the side of his head as he attempted to grab her. He staggered and crashed back, tripped over one of the upturned chairs and collapsed, semi-conscious onto the floor.

Ellie was terrified. She stood up and glanced at him. He showed signs of awaking and she knew that if he did she might not even survive the attack.

She stepped around him, tore into the bedroom and grabbed the already half-packed bag she had placed weekend clothes in. She tossed some extra work clothes in, zipped it up and headed to her car. It was parked beside Jaxon's in the garage. She opened the automatic doors and reversed out.

As she swung her car around in the driveway, the house door opened and Jaxon came out, shouting incoherently as he ran towards her.

If he reached her...

Ellie became calmer and managed to avoid hitting him with the car. She saw him in her rear vision mirror light under the glare of a streetlight actually attempting to keep up as she accelerated away.

Her throbbing head cleared a little as she drove on but where could she go?

A few moments later she arrived at a tiny immaculately kept townhouse and drove into the driveway. The interior lights were on so she knew someone was there.

She staggered out of the car as pain hit her body and rang the front door bell.

The door opened and a surprised looking Janice Pringle stood there.

"Oh my God, Ellie," she said and reached out to her. "What happened?'

"Can you help me please," Ellie cried. "Jaxon attacked me."

Her DP and the doorway began to spin but she was safe. She attempted to stay conscious but failed with her last recollection being that of Janice seizing her in a warm embrace and guiding her inside.

"AND YOU NEVER TOLD a soul?" Janice said after she bandaged up Ellie's arm. The wound had probably been caused by the broken plate and wasn't too deep.

'This is the worst he has ever been," Ellie replied. "It's been going on more or less since I was appointed to the principal's position at our school."

"But why? I would have thought he'd be proud of you."

"Male chauvinistic pride. I earn almost double his salary and his attempts to get promotion never get anywhere. He's a sales consultant with one of those warehouses that imports and distributes clothing and similar domestic products." Ellie grimaced. "It gives him an excuse to be away from home several times a month."

"I know the sort," Janice replied. "Anyway, you can stay here the night and longer if you wish. Perhaps you could take tomorrow off."

"Thanks Janice. I will stay the night but still go off to Riversdale for the weekend." She stopped and pouted. "When I overruled you at school today there was nothing personal, you know."

"You have that ability I'd never have. I just get angry and end up acting like an old sergeant major in the army," Janice replied with a shrug. "I was thinking about what you proposed earlier and actually think that idea of having two parallel Year 3 to 6 classes has merit. We can divide the ratbags up..." She continued on talking about school life and said no more about the attack. This was appreciated more by Ellie than if it was dwelt upon.

THOUGH STILL FEELING quite sore in the ribs, Ellie found that Friday began well. Even her brief announcement to the staff about the immediate changes was accepted. Both Janice and Kerenza radiated a mature and professional attitude. For perhaps the first time in weeks, they chatted with each other in the staffroom at morning interval about everyday things.

Thomas Road School was like a real home for her and in complete contrast to her domestic situation. Ellie was, though determined to leave Jaxon and not relent. It was too late to save their marriage now.

AT THE END OF THE LUNCH hour, there were two bells five minutes apart. The first was for everyone playing sport or just having fun at the far end of the playing field to pack up, change out of sports clothes if necessary and bring any gear in. The second bell was to go to classes ready for the afternoon.

Ellie usually spent the Friday afternoon doing administrative work in her office and was there when Janice walked in.

"Karl hasn't returned to class," Janice said. "Nicky the duty teacher said she had broken up a fight between him and a couple of other boys in my room."

Karl was one of those timid little boys who wasn't very sporty and would rather just sit around reading a book than play rugby that most of the senior boys did during the lunch hour. It was unusual for him to be involved in any fights.

"That's unusual," Ellie said. "Did Nicky know what the fight was about?"

"Something that isn't related to school. Gerard and Colin were teasing him and he struck out."

Gerard and Colin were two problem pupilss in the senior school.

"So what happened?"

"They stopped fighting when Nicky asked so she did no more about it. Other boys in my class said they saw Karl heading out the back gate after the first in bell."

"Could he have gone home?"

"That's the problem. Both his parents work and nobody would be there. I called his place but nobody answered the landline. We don't have a record of any family mobile number."

"If it wasn't for the fight I wouldn't be so worried," Janice said. "Karl hasn't been himself all week but only this morning said he was okay. However, I think something is wrong at home."

"Okay, I'll follow it up. Thanks."

"Ellie looked up Karl's address. It was about three kilometres away and out of their school zone. There were about fifty pupils from out of their catchment area at Thomas Road School. His notes stated that he took a city bus to and from school every day. This was not unusual as the bus company had what were really school buses that fitted in with their hours. However, there were none at this time of the day. Also the back school gate just led in a suburban street and was well away from the bus route.

She told Teresa, her office assistant what she was going to do and drove her car around the block to reach the back of the school grounds. She stopped had a brief look around and saw a woman doing a garden nearby. The woman confirmed that she had seen a boy come out and pointed up the road to her left. Ellie frowned for she would have headed in the opposite direction towards Karl's home. She thanked her and headed towards the city centre where the woman pointed.

Three blocks later she have a sigh of relief for she recognised Karl walking along the footpath at quite a steady pace as if he knew where he was going. She drove past him, pulled to the kerb, climbed out of her car and waited as Karl approached.

He almost banged into her before he realised who she was.

"Mrs Parkes!" he gasped and looked around as if he was contemplating making a dash across the road.

"Just stop, Karl," Ellie said in a kind voice. "I only want to talk."

He looked up at her and tears filled his eyes. "They were teasing me and said that Mum was going to leave Dad and me but she wouldn't do that would she? I'm going to her office in High Street."

Ellie walked a few steps to her car and opened the front door for him. "Just sit in my car, shall we?"

"I'm in trouble aren't I otherwise you wouldn't be out looking for me?"

"When you didn't come to afternoon class Miss Prindle was worried about you, Karl but you are not in trouble."

"Colin said that Mum was going to move in with his dad and he'd be his Mum from now on."

Ellie knew that Colin lived with his father and a so-called housekeeper. There were a few dysfunctional families with children at the school and they kept a list of children who might need that extra support. Colin's home life was one of the worse.

"So we'll go and find your Mum shall we?" she said and started the car.

"Won't Miss Prindle be mad at me?"

"I doubt it," Ellie said as they drove off.

Karl looked at her and gave a slight grin. "But you're her boss, aren't you? If you say it's okay she can't do anything about it."

Ellie smiled to herself. "Something like that," she said.

Under Karl's direction they stopped at an office block at the edge of the commercial buildings.

"Can you come in?" Karl asked. "Mum's going to be mad at me for wagging school."

"Sure," Ellie replied. "Lead the way."

Ellie vaguely knew Karl's mother, Jessie Watson but she hadn't had a lot to do with her. She appeared to be a receptionist in the office they arrived at.

"Karl! What are you doing here?" She looked up and saw Ellie. "Mrs Parkes, what's wrong? Is Karl ill?"

"A little distressed, that's all," Ellie replied.

"About last night, wasn't it Karl?" Jessie looked across at Ellie and looked embarrassed. "My husband and I had an argument after Karl went to bed. He must have overheard everything."

"Possibly," Ellie said. "It's none of my business, of course but he thought you might be leaving him. Some of the boys in his class were tormenting him."

"Colin said you were going to move in with his dad and leave Dad and me." Karl burst into tears, "I don't want that to happen."

Jessie stepped out and grabbed her son in a massive hug, "Oh Sweetheart it wasn't that at all. It's true that your dad and me had a row last night after you went to bed but that was all. Those boys just made a up a story to tease you."

"And they won't do it again," Ellie said. "If either of them bully you or anybody else again they'll be banned from playing in next month's inter-school winter sports tournament."

Karl looked up at his mother. "And Mrs Parkes can do that, Mum. Even Miss Pringle has to do what she says."

After Ellie left Karl with his mother and drove back to school she grimaced. It was a pity that her own problems couldn't be solved so easily.

CHAPTER 3

Jaxon Parkes cursed when the tracer he had on Ellie's mobile cut out earlier that day. It appeared that she had driven out of range but why had she taken a road that led nowhere except a remote beach and a handful of farms? She'd told him in no uncertain terms that she was going to Riversdale for a few days to gather her thoughts.

His recollection of the previous night was a blur. Oh there was that inevitable argument about him coming home late after a time at the pub with his friends. She was so wrapped up in her job she never bothered to accompany him, not like when they first met and she was delighted in joining in the fun. Now, it was all that damned school that took up all her time and was all she could talk about. Mind you, her salary was twice as much as he earned and their house was just about mortgage free.

Silly bitch wasn't even that good in bed any more. Always too tired or had a 'let's get it over with' attitude when he cuddled up. No wonder he sort out other women for companionship.

He cursed and drank the last third of the can of beer as he drove through the misty rain along the gravel road after the seal had stopped. But why had she become so antagonistic?

He could guess of course. It was probably that Brian Fleming, that oh so slimy Board Of Trustees chairman she always talked about who always supported her when she wanted something for the school. He owned half the town and his wife was one of those nutters who spent all her time at one of those leftie charities. From what he'd heard they only stayed together because of their snobby kids.

Ellie was probably off to spend the weekend in one of Fleming's beach houses. Oh she could still turn on the charm when she wanted something. Fleming would be turned on by her figure that, he had to admit was still pretty good. Compared with Ellie, Fleming's wife was overweight and over made up. He'd hardly ever seen the woman in casual clothes.

Jaxon flung the now empty beer can over onto the back seat and cursed all women. He grimaced as he stared out through wipers attempting to cope with the downpour and remembered a little about what had happened. Oh the silly bitch deserved the little thump he'd given her when she had a cold meal awaiting when he arrived home.

And then that story about wanting to spend the weekend at Riversdale Beach alone to think about their future. Yeah right! Meeting up with Fleming was more like it.

And now he was on this damn back road trying to find her. He would, too and she'd learn how to be a faithful wife and cater for his needs. Being a bloody school principal was fine for the income she got but it shouldn't be everything in their lives.

He grinned and reached for another can of beer. If it wasn't for her job he'd have never met Salem Milne, a young teacher at the school. She was everything Ellie used to be and in bed was much like his wife was years ago. She was visiting her parents in Auckland over the weekend.

"Bitch," he spat after wiping beer froth off his lips. He wasn't sure what woman he referred to for his affair with Salem was becoming a pain, too. Damn women always started off okay then they wanted everything done their way.

Jaxon drove over a rise and saw the road wind down through grass-covered hills. The rain had almost stopped but he realised why his tracer on Ellie's mobile had stopped. His mobile now showed that there was no signal. Oh well, she must be somewhere ahead for there had been no side roads for several kilometres. His dashboard map showed only one farmhouse ahead and a dozen or so buildings, probably summer batches across the road from a small beach that was tucked in between cliffs overlooking the ocean. That was it for the road went no further.

Ten minutes later he drove around a corner and cursed. Ahead was a raging stream and the bridge had gone! He pulled onto a grassy area nearby and grabbed his coat. The road was narrow and he wanted to examine the grass further in to see whether it could support his car if he attempted to turn around.

It appeared to be okay but he decided to have a look around by the bridge. That stream was certainly a raging torrent. He squinted out and noticed something red on the far side. Oh hell, it was Ellie's car that was upside down amongst debris from the bridge.

What if she was inside?

But what could he do? There was no way he could get across the stream to reach the car. He'd better turn around, drive back up the hill until his mobile worked and call for help.

He was about to do that when he saw a Land Cruiser appear around a bend on the far side. It braked and he could easily see the driver get out. By his clothes, he looked like a local farmer who'd probably come to inspect the road.

"Bloody hell," he swore for a woman opened the passenger door and also stepped out.

It was Ellie! She wasn't in her car after all. His relief turned to jealousy and rage. Why was she with this other guy and also why was she dressed in a top and jeans that made her look like an old farmer's wife?

The bitch! So that's what was why she was on this road in the first place. She was having an affair with a local farmer and had arranged to spend the weekend with him. This guy probably had a beach cottage out here.

It all fitted in! Here she was screwing one of the parents from her school and had arranged this sexy weekend with him. It wasn't Fleming after all but this other bastard! And he was worried about her being in her car a few moments earlier.

She'd parked her car near the stream and kept going with this other guy. The flood arrived and swept the parked car away. He swore and vowed that he wasn't going to allow her to do this.

But what could he do! When he got to her he'd show her! He clenched his fists as he watched the Land Cruiser reverse up the road and disappear out of sight.

The flooded stream was too rough to cross over now but these flash floods never lasted long. If he couldn't get in they couldn't get out. He would also leave but not bother to call for help when he was in mobile range. This was something he had to tend to himself and by God; she'd regret everything she had done.

He laughed sarcastically.No wonder she was so useless in bed. She'd probably been shacking up with this guy for months. He stormed back to his car, almost got it stuck in the soft grass as he reversed around with the wheels spinning. Luckily he managed to find firm ground and headed back. Already thoughts were going through his mind about how he would solve this problem. So his always loyal wife was just a slut like all the other bitches around!

He'd show her! He's show them all including Salem Milne. There were plenty of other attractive women around. He didn't need these two. Not at all!

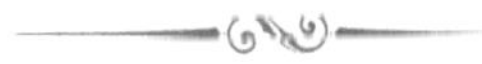

JAXON'S MOBILE CAME on line at the top of the hill on the way back. He switched to the remote speaker as he drove and called Ellie. As expected though, there was no response so he selected preselect number seven,

"Hello, Salem speaking," came the almost sleepy voice. "Is that you, Jaxon?"

"Sure is." At least her voice cheered him up. "How's it going in Auckland?"

"Didn't get there," she replied. "All flights were cancelled due to the storm so I stayed in town."

Wow. That was better. He'd visit her and at least have a pleasant night with the normal benefits. Damn Ellie!

"That's great. I'm out of town with Ellie at the moment but will be back this evening," he said over the mobile. "As you probably know, she's going to some principals meeting," The lies just ran off his tongue as he laughed. "She can't even get away from work in the weekends."

There was hesitation in Salem's voice before she replied. "Can't do it tonight I'm... err...afraid. My younger sister is in town and is staying over for the week. Remember I told you about Lyanna."

He vaguely remembered her mentioning a younger sister who had recently returned from Australia. He grinned. Now if she was anything as attractive as Salem, it might be a good chance to get to know her.

"So I'll take you both out. Isn't that live show in town that you wanted to see? We could have a meal and."

"Can't." Salem sounded hesitant again after he had finished talking.

What followed made his mind jolt!

"Who is it on the phone, Sal?" He heard a male voice in the background before the contact became mute.

Salem came back on line a few seconds later "Sorry Jaxon. I can't do it. We need to talk about things. I'll call you in a couple of days. See you!"

The call was disconnected.

My God, she was giving him the brush off! And who was the guy? The bitch. How dare she! He slammed the off button and almost ran off the narrow road as he swallowed anger. Both the bitches were screwing other men. After everything he'd done for them. In Salem's case he had paid off a credit card bill for her after she had agreed to sleep with him. That had turned into a full affair that had been going on for three months now.

He pressed redial but only got Salem's voice mail. So now she refused to answer her mobile. Cowardly bitch! He'd show her too!

He roared on far too fast for the road conditions and just about failed to take a tight corner. He braked, swung back across the road and decided that he'd better slow down. His car was excellent on city streets but wasn't made for these horrible country roads. Why anyone would want to actually live out here in the wilds was beyond him.

IT WAS EARLY EVENING but pitch dark on a typical winter's day when Jaxon arrived outside Salem's place, a small apartment in an old somewhat run down over a century old villa She lived alone but told him she was looking for someone else to share the rent with. He'd even helped her pay the rent last month and now; he glowered and shrugged when he noticed her car in her allocated car park. At least she was home.

As he normally did over the last few weeks he just strolled in but didn't call out as usual. There was a light in the living room up the corridor but the door was shut. Then he heard her laughter and distinct sound of stools being shifted. He pushed the door open and blinked in the bright light.

There before him lying, not sitting on the couch was Salem. She reached out to a nearby coffee table and picked up a wine glass. He gasped for the blouse she often wore: one of those frilly white ones was three quarters undone exposing her skimpy bra.

"Your wine's poured, Lucas," she cooed before she turned and noticed that who was standing there. "Jaxon! What are you doing here?"

"You two timing bitch!" Jaxon snarled. He stepped forward and grabbed for her but she screamed and ducked beneath his outstretched hand.

Jaxon heard a sound behind him and saw a massive guy charge in through the door he'd just entered. In that split second he noticed how huge the guy was, one of those rugby forwards type and weighing over ninety kilograms of bulging muscles.

"No you don't, mate," the guy snarled and grabbed Jaxon in a grip so tight that he flinched with pain. He was swung around and fierce eyes stared at him, mere centimetres from his face. "Is this the guy who has been annoying you, Sal?"

"Not really," Salem almost whispered and watched as Lucas stepped back from him. "He's just my boss's husband."

She stared at Jaxon, sort of sucked on her bottom lip and blinked a couple of times as if she wanted him to follow her story up.

"You're a lying bitch," Jaxon snarled and turned to the intruder. "She's my partner Mate so whatever you thought about doing this evening, just forget about it and get out!"

"Is she now," Lucas whispered. "And you storm in and would have attacked her if I hadn't been here." He stepped forward and Jaxon cowered back when he suddenly realised that he could be in danger.

"It wasn't like that," he stuttered. "I just..."

Lucas pushed him none too gently on the shoulder. "Now, what did you just call Sal, my friend?" he said in a tone that was anything except friendly.

"Just leave him, Lucas," Salem's bottom lip shook. "We did have a date a couple of times and..."

"A couple of times!" Jaxon screamed forgetting the guy before him in that moment of anger.

"No, he's not worth it," cried Salem

Jaxon caught a glimpse of a fist heading his way but there was no way to avoid it. He felt himself being propelled backwards across the room and pain across his mouth. There was blood, his blood and excruciating pain as he shook his head and spat out salvia. His head hit something as everything around began to spin He found himself hauled up by his collar and a second fist pounded him in the face. He reeled back, heard a distinct crack as he again hit something by the wall and crashed to his knees. He staggered, saw has attacker looming over him and felt a violent kick in the ribs.

He groaned and remembered vague voices that sounded like Salem pleading Lucas to stop, another kick in the ribs then ... nothing as he lost consciousness.

"STOP IT," SCREAMED Salem. "He's had enough. Just leave him!"

Lucas stood back and stretched his fingers out as if he was trying to restore circulation in his hand. "He would have done something worse with you if I hadn't arrived," he panted.

"Okay, but he's hit his head on the side of the bookshelf. He's out cold and there's blood everywhere."

"Just a nose bleed," Lucas muttered. "Nothing worse than what one would get in a rugby scrum. He'd come around soon."

"He won't," Salem retorted, "Look at his eyes." They were sort of all rolled up under his eyelids. "'Get some help. My God, did you have to be so violent. He's half your size."

"Okay! Okay," Lucas muttered and reached for his mobile. "Hello, there's been a bit of a fight with an attacker at my girlfriend's place.... Yes... yes... I'll wait." He glanced at Salem and repeated everything again to another operator, gave her their address and listened to instructions before he clicked off.

"So what's happening?' Salem asked.

"An ambulance will be here in twenty minutes or so. Meanwhile we should just cover him with a blanket but don't try to shift him." Lucas tucked his arms gently around her. "Sorry Sal but I'm pretty sure he was about to attack you."

Salem stared up at him. "He was. He's done it before and I was about to break it up with him." She burst into tears and stepped back. "I'll get a blanket."

"Yeah," Lucas replied. "Don't worry. The ambulance will be here soon."

CHAPTER 4

Around four in afternoon the sun had already fallen behind the western hills and the temperature had dropped. The storm was almost over. According to the radio that was tuned to an AM station as FM was out of range, more was coming up from the south.

Ellie dressed in a warm coat, again borrowed from Wyatt's ex, climbed out of the Land Cruiser and gazed at the bridge scene. The water had fallen but was still quite high and she could see her car downstream looking grotesque with the wheels in the air.

"We can now ford the stream in that up-steam section that doesn't look too bad," Wyatt said as he stood beside her. "It's still quite swift but won't come up above the tyres."

To Ellie it still looked dangerous. "And will the water drop any further?" she asked.

"Sure but I wouldn't want to attempt crossing in the dark."

"And tomorrow?"

Wyatt shrugged. "Hard to tell. If that southerly comes up again there could be another flood. If it holds off until tomorrow morning as the radio suggests it should be almost down to its normal size for this time of the year. The ford has a concrete base and was designed for large trucks too heavy for the bridge."

Ellie turned to him and grinned. "So if you wouldn't mind, I'd rather stay for another night rather than tempt fate too much."

Wyatt grinned. "You wish is my command, Madam," he said and gave a bow with one arm across his chest and the other extended out wide.

Ellie smiled. Wyatt was a bit of a character with that sense of humour. It was strange but she felt comforted by his actions.

"Come on Cinders," Wyatt called for the dog had also jumped out of the vehicle and had dashed away to sniff at everything around.

Cinders arrived back soaking wet and shook himself before Ellie. She laughed and rubbed his ears. "Did you have to pick right before me to do that?"

With everyone aboard they headed back with the headlights on as darkness had dropped over the silent land. When they arrived Ellie noticed a small light showing on the side of the house."

"Security lights in the kitchen," Wyatt explained. "It comes on in at night but goes off at random times between nine and midnight and on about seven in the morning if it's still dark. One comes on in an upstairs bedroom later. It's better than an outside light blazing away outside to actually make the place seem empty."

"Great idea." Ellie said. "Did you design it?"

"I did actually," Wyatt said. "Sold a few copies to locals for their farms and cottages. I enjoy fiddling around with electronics. Different from my work in town."

Ellie smiled. The house looked so welcoming and secure. It was almost as if she had known it for years and not just the last day. Perhaps it was the company she was with? What a contrast Wyatt was to Jaxon and his moody ways. Thinking back, Jaxon had once been everything she had had hoped for. It was a pity that he had taken to drink after a few work setbacks and blamed her for practically everything. Perhaps not having children hadn't helped.

A sloppy nose poked into her arm and she glanced back to see Cinders gazing at her.

"You've made a friend for life," Wyatt said as he drove into a large shed behind the house. "Want to help make a meal? I've got lots of stuff in the deep freeze that is mainly home grown or fresh meat. They always give me some from the farm, I guess to thank me for the small rent I charge for the few acres I lease them."

"Sounds wonderful," Ellie responded as she slipped the wet coat off and hung it on a nearby hook.

The meal went well with far too much cooked but Ellie placed the extra food in containers to go in the nearby deep freeze. Afterwards she was interested in watchung a couple of renovation disks Wyatt put on the television. He was quite keen on redoing the kitchen and living area.

"Jennifer wanted the bedrooms done first and two of them were upgraded last year." He grinned. "The en suite bathrooms for both rooms were too expensive so you still have to use that bathroom along the hallway, I'm afraid."

"It's no problem. Those older bathrooms are quite large compared with newer ones."

It was now close to eleven and after washing the last dishes as Wyatt dried and put everything away she said goodnight and headed for her bedroom.

MORNING ARRIVED AFTER what could have been Ellie's best sleep in years. She had slept right through with no horrible dreams that usually punctured her thoughts. Jaxon, school and everything else that had been worrying now seemed to be in perspective. Her bedroom door was shut but there was a scratching outside.

"Hi Cinders," she said when the dog bounded in after she opened the door. "Did Wyatt sent you to awaken me? I guess I should have left the door ajar for you last night."

Big mournful eyes gazed up at her but a wagging tail showed that he was glad to be with her. She dressed in newly found clothes and walked downstairs to that now familiar aroma of a country breakfast.

"Hi, Wyatt," she said. "I slept in, I'm afraid."

"So what? Aren't weekends for that?"

He handed her a repeat of yesterday's massive breakfast, poured coffee into a mug and sat by her at the breakfast nook. The chat about the house continued and switched to herself and school life. Neither Jaxon nor Jennifer were mentioned and everything was so positive that she glanced at him.

"So we're both achieving what a break is all about?"

He grinned. "Yes. Out here the world can be ignored. The weather is more important than all the crime and doom talked about in news programs. I actually gave up watching the television news months ago. Who cares when some politician moans on about something?"

Ellie sighed. "True but it is still out there." She caught his eye. "So we'll be able to ford the river, today?"

"It'll be no problem. The storm never arrived, I can get you home today if you wish." He frowned. "I'll be heading back too." He sort of looked sheepish. "Would you like to come and visit again, sometime? No restrictions or commitments but just a chance to get away from the hassles of our respective lives."

Ellie smiled and avoided his eyes. "Thank you. I'd love to return." She laughed. "No surf rescues, wrecked cars or second hand clothes, though." Her smile turned to concern. "Can I show you something?"

"Sure."

She took off the log-sleeved jersey. She had chosen a short-sleeved top so her arms were now bare and showed several bruises. Without another word she lifted her top slightly to show her torso and two massive bruises. "I told you a little about Jaxon. The stomach wound are when he kicked me when I was on the floor."

"You aren't going back to him after this," Wyatt almost spat. "Anybody who does this to a partner should be arrested for domestic violence. Have you reported him to the police?"

She shook her head. "I thought I could cope and it was just a rough patch he was going through."

Wyatt grimaced. "But now?"

"The reason I booked that weekend cottage in Riversdale was to get away and just think. Now, here I am moaning away about my problems to you."

"And I'll help you. That's a promise!"

He stood up stepped forward and gripped her in an affectionate cuddle. But that was it. There was nothing else, no kiss or sexual overtures. There was just an affectionate hug that was all she needed at that time.

He grinned and stepped back. "It'll take an hour or so to pack up but that works out well. When the tide is out the stream will be lower and easier to ford so perhaps after lunch will be an even better time to leave."

Ellie nodded. "Suits me. If I had arrived at Riversdale, I'd still be there so nobody is expecting me back until tomorrow, you know school staff and so forth?"

"We could take a walk along the beach with Cinders. He loves the surf and the waves have also gone down. Even the winter sun has a little warmth in it."

A LITTLE AFTER NOON they were back at the bridge itself that looked similar to the view during the flood. The water level was completely different and back to an almost normal level. In Wyatt's view it was not too bad for fording. Downstream, Ellie's car had shifted a little and was now on the side and squeezed into a large tree trunk with swirling water around.

"I wouldn't go near it," Wyatt warned. "Often holes are scoured out and you could get trapped. Leave it to your insurance company to retrieve. I'm sure they'll just write it off and you can buy a new one."

Ellie shrugged. "There was just my suitcase and iPad. My clothes and so forth would be ruined and anything on my iPad is also on the school computer."

She was nervous as Wyatt drove the Land Cruiser into the water and to her, the water level was high and almost to the bottom of the door. Wyatt though, just grinned and drove slowly forward, water seemed to just slide by as they approached the far bank and finally up the other side to rejoin the road.

She sighed and caught his eyes, "Thanks. I'm glad it was you driving."

"You just take it steady and keep going. I've seen these young guys roar in with water splashing everywhere and end up in the middle with a stalled engine."

Cinders in his usual place in the back barked in agreement and stared out with his tail wagging.

"I know, Cinders," Ellie said with a laugh. "It's all part of the fun, isn't it?"

At the summit of the next hill her iPhone chirped and the screen lit up.

There were fifteen unanswered calls and twenty-three messages. She grimaced and was about read the messages when the mobile chirped to indicate a call was there.

"Hello Ellie speaking," she said.

A woman's distressed voice was almost sobbing as she talked.

"I've been trying to get you since yesterday," she sobbed. "Lucas had a fight with Jaxon who tried to attack me. Jaxon's in the Hutt Hospital and is pretty badly beaten up."

Ellie frowned. Who was this Lucas guy? Also, she still hadn't worked out who was speaking. She was obviously stressed out.

"Just take it slowly... err..."

"It's Salem!"

Of course she should have recognised her voice but when someone is sobbing... But why would she be the one calling her?

"Just take it slowly, Salem. I'm in mobile range and I am heading home."

She pressed the speaker button so Wyatt could hear the conversation.

Salem's voice became more coherent as everything came out... everything from the affair she was having with Jaxon to the latest episode where her present boyfriend, the Lucas guy stopped her from being attacked by Jaxon.

IT WAS LUNCHTIME BEFORE they arrived at Ellie's home. It looked no different, of course, but she found her sense of anguish had diminished. She glanced across at Wyatt who appeared quite serious. Even Cinders on the back seat seemed to sense a tension and just looked out the window with his tail drooped.

"Nice place," Wyatt said as they pulled into the drive.

"It was," Ellie responded. "My parents paid the deposit a few years back and the mortgage is in my name. I've paid Mum and Dad back and have half the mortgage ..." She talked on about her place for a few moments. Finally she opened the car door and smiled at him. "Well come in. At least we can have a coffee together."

Wyatt looked embarrassed. "I don't want to just drive off into the sunset," he said. "Even Cinders will miss you."

She sat back down in the car seat and stared at him. He looked so earnest and... oh hell, she didn't know what to think. "So what do you want, Wyatt? I'm not just that stranded woman you rescued from the surf, you know. I've got hang ups and problems." She laughed. "Fancy, one of my teacher's screwing my husband, he has been unfaithful for years and my car's a write off. How's that for a start?"

"And I have an ex who is hell bent in getting everything." He grinned. "It's only the lawyers who make a profit."

"So?" She asked.

"I want to see you again. We can support each other." He reached across, grabbed her hands and kissed her lightly on the cheek. He squeezed her hands before shuffling back and reaching for his own door. "A coffee, you said?"

Ellie grinned. "Yeah and I can even find something for Cinders to munch."

WYATT INSISTED ON DRIVING Ellie to Hutt Hospital but agreed to wait in the carpark rather than going in with her. Afterwards they would go the car rental firm where her insurance company arranged for her to pick up a rental car. The company had also arranged to have Ellie's old car salvaged from the river.

When she walked along the corridor to the ward where her husband was she saw Salem approach. The young woman gave a small gasp but there was no retreat. She stopped but couldn't look Ellie in the eyes.

Ellie reached out and squeezed Salem's arm. "It is okay," she said. "I know what Jaxon is like. Did it all start at last year's staff Christmas do?"

Salem looked up with tears in her eyes. "It was almost blackmail," she whispered. "I had too much to drink and ..." Tears rolled down her cheeks. "I'll have my resignation in your office on Monday morning."

"And I will reject it," Ellie replied.

Salem finally looked up and caught Ellie's eyes. "But why? I've had an affair with Jaxon for all of this year"

"So? If it wasn't you, he would have had one with someone else, probably more than one. If every staff member who has had some sort of fling while teaching at our school was fired, quarter of the staff would be gone. I know you spend most of Sunday down at our school. Even Helene Edwards, the most complaining parent we have, said how pleased she was with Bryan in your room."

Salem wiped her eyes. "He is a handful," she admitted.

"So just move on in life. Jaxon is not worth it. How is Lucas, anyway?"

Salem shrugged. "Okay, I guess."

"Whatever," Ellie replied. "It is none of my business anyway but remember if you want any help about anything, not just school stuff, just ask."

Salem nodded. "I told Jaxon it was finished but I guess he realised that anyway. His wounds are not too bad now and he should be released from hospital tomorrow." She grinned. "His face is a bit bruised."

Ellie stepped forward with her arms out. "So give me a hug and no more talk of resigning. Okay?"

The hug was a tight one before Salem stood back, smiled almost shyly, said a brief 'bye and left. Ellie grimaced. That was one minor concern fixed but now came the real challenge for she was about to tell Jaxon that their marriage was over. Determined to do it now, she almost strutted into the adjacent ward.

JAXON WAS SITTING UP in bed having a coffee when Ellie walked in. His face was puffed up in a massive bruise and his left eye was a mere slit.

"Come to gloat?" were his first words.

Ellie just stood there with a faint smile across her face.

"Well, can't you say anything?" he snapped.

"Oh I could say plenty, Jaxon but what is the use?" she almost whispered. "I put up with you for years now. It actually ended between us years ago but I clung on and at times, even blaming myself." She stared down at him. "I'm moving out so won't be in our home. The house is in our name and I've been paying the mortgage for years now. You can have a choice, either buy me out of my half and take over the mortgage or move out yourself. I'm sure our lawyers will come to an agreement."

She waited for an angry outburst but he just stared at her, almost like a frightened little boy who had been sent to her office by a frustrated teacher.

"Oh I mean it," Ellie continued forgetting the promise to say no more. "I'm filing a legal separation with my lawyer and a restraining order against you. When I'm at my new place, if you come within two hundred metres of it, my lawyer will be directed to file criminal assault charges against you including rape, if necessary."

"Oh don't be an idiot." Jaxon appeared to get his confidence back again. "We're married so you'll be laughed all of the way out of the courtroom."

"In the 1960s possibly but not now." Ellie glowered. "Stacey told me everything, too. Heard her new boyfriend, that huge guy, was the one who belted you up. Now, what's his name?" She snapped her fingers. "Lucas, nice guy I hear, but a bit short tempered. A bit like you, I think. "

"Bitch!" Jaxon spat.

"Who, Salem, myself or those other young women you've screwed this year? Yes, I know about most of them, too." Ellie gave a sarcastic smile. "Goodbye Jaxon. Stop drinking, grow up and watch that temper of yours"

She turned and without a backward glance, walked out of the ward.

CHAPTER 5

After climbing in the Land Cruiser, Ellie almost slammed the passenger door shut.

"So how did it go?" Wyatt asked.

"Don't ask!" she almost spat and glared out the windscreen. She turned and noticed his concerned look. "I blew it actually and forgot everything about being in control of my emotions."

"It's okay," Wyatt replied. "But if you'd like to talk about it, I'm all ears.

"He hasn't changed," Ellie muttered and told him everything that she'd said to Jaxon.

Wyatt grinned. "So you're really going to move out?"

Ellie shrugged. "I have to, I guess. If I stay home he is capable of doing anything. Guess I can go home to my mother's place for a while. She's a widow who lives in Wellington. Dad died a few years back." She glowered out the windscreen.

"Problem's there, too?"

Ellie turned and stared into his eyes. "Oh Mum's okay. It's just that neither her or Dad approved of my marriage to Jaxon and she is inclined to say 'Told you so' that doesn't help the situation."

"I'll see what I can do," Wyatt said. "We have several apartments or rental properties on our books." He grinned. "You'd be amazed about how many women approach us wanting a place more or less straight away. Most are at the end of their tether and have children with them."

"You can help? I can't commit myself to any long term contract until things are sorted."

"Sure," He took out his mobile and Ellie heard a woman's voice on his speaker.

"Hi Cynthia," Wyatt said. "You know that block of apartments above that closed shop in High Street, Lower Hutt. Are any still available for rental?"

"I'll check." There was a sound of keyboard clicking and her voice returned. 'There are the three new ones ready. We're all set to advertise them in next week's advertising campaign. I'm sure they'll be popular."

"And can we get a short term contract?"

"Possibly," Cynthia replied.

"Right. Check it out. I may have a client."

"Will do."

Wyatt clicked off. "That was my secretary. She's sixty of she's a day but is pretty spot on when it comes to the best deals in town. The owner has converted an old office building into half a dozen apartments. They are above three shops and have a basement car park. Interested?"

Ellie gasped. "Oh my God. It's all so sudden, I don't know."

HOWEVER, WITH WYATT'S help, Ellie shifted into a small modern apartment above the main shopping centre in Lower Hutt three days later after two nights in a motel. She had brought furniture from her old place mainly from their second bedroom and about half the living room and kitchen furniture and utensils as well as her remaining personal stuff. Karenza, had been a great help with her shift. Luckily Jaxon had chosen not to confront her when the packers arrived after her lawyer had informed him about the times involved. In fact, she had had no contact with her husband what-so-ever since she'd left him at the hospital but she still had that uneasy feeling that he wasn't too far away.

Their floor and her own apartment had an alarm system and the basement carpark was secure with spaces for vehicles of the apartment tenants and the chemist shop and a coffee bar workers on the street level below. The apartments were accessed though a central corridor and a lift to the ground floor and basement. Again this was secure with codes necessary to use it. The stairs also had a secure door at street level onto a small alleyway between their building and the store next door. Everything was well lit at night and Ellie felt far safer there than she would have been back in her old home.

Back at Thomas Road School after morning interval there was a knock on her door and a sheepish looking Salem stood there. As with the other younger teachers, Salem had a half-day release from classroom duties that included a short time with herself. She seemed to be making a huge effort to please her in any way possible.

"I've tried to do everything right, you know," Salem said.

Ellie smiled. "Too much so, Salem. You don't have to prove anything to me or anyone else. Just be yourself and relax."

"Was it my fault you moved out from Jaxon?" Salem whispered after she sat down.

"You know it wasn't. I thought I'd explained it all to you."

"He came back," Salem whispered... "Well, you can guess." She lifted up the bottom of blouse she was wearing to show a massive bruise across her midriff. "He got aggressive and blamed me for your marriage breakdown."

"When?" Ellie gasped.

"Last night." Salem's lips trembled as she continued the account of what had happened.

IT WAS MID-EVENING and Salem had a pile of classroom projects spread across the kitchen table. This was her second year at Thomas Road School and she had been allocated a Year 4 class of nine-year-old children rather than the six year olds in Year 2 the year before. One disadvantage was that the children produced far more sophisticated written work. She felt proud of this work they were doing and felt it was necessary to read and comment of every child's effort. This now involved working at home.

The knock on the door made her jerk up for she must have dropped off. She frowned but was unconcerned; probably Isabella across the road had locked herself out, yet again. Though friendly and bright she was always doing this, hence the key left with her at times like this.

"Coming," she called.

However, as soon as she turned the lock it was flung open and Jaxon stormed in. Oh hell, she could see from his face that he was in a foul mood. He grabbed her arm and almost dragged her across to a couch, There he flung her onto it and stood before her,

"Okay, what do you want, Jaxon?" she said in an enforced calm voice. She knew shouting at him to leave would be of no value.

"Ellie! Where does she live?" he spat. "And don't tell me you don't know."

"She doesn't want to see you. Take my advice and..."

Jaxon reached forward, seized her arm and dragged her up in front of him. "You will tell me, you stupid bitch!"

He was so close she could smell the beer on his breath She struggled and received a slap across the face. It hurt!

She staggered back, lost her footing and ended up on the floor. Bile rose in her throat as she frantically attempted to roll sideways. However, she was too slow and received a kick in the stomach. She was grabbed by the neck and found she couldn't breathe as she was dragged up.

Luckily, her attacker let her go with a violent shove back onto the couch. She kicked out, heard him mutter an oath and took the chance to duck beneath an incoming punch. Now on all fours, she screamed and attempted to escape.

But he was too strong! She was held in a vice like group, frog marched through to the adjacent bedroom and flung on the bed.

In some ways this helped for her mobile was within reach. Still kicking she reached out and managed to press a button; which one, she had no idea.

Rational thoughts returned. "I wouldn't try any thing, Jaxon," she said in a mere whisper. "That was Lucas I called. His place is only five minutes away and I know he's home. If you're still here when he arrives ..."

It worked.

Jaxon's aggression changed to fear.

"Bitch," he retorted. "Just tell Ellie that nobody tries to get the better of Jaxon Parkes, not even her or that fancy lawyer she employs. She'd better watch her back!"

He turned and retreated. Gasping for breath, Salem heard the front door slam. She rushed out, slid the night latch across, sank to the floor and burst into tears.

"THAT WAS QUICK THINKING," Ellie praised. "But you said you didn't know if you got Lucas on your mobile."

"It was all a bluff," Salem replied. "I don't go out with Lucas any more and anyway he lives right across town."

"Jaxon is a typical cowardly bully," Ellie said. "I'm glad the threat worked."

"But you're in danger, Ellie," Salem said. "He's just going to ignore any restrictions imposed on him. All he needs to do is follow your car home and it won't take long for him to find your new place."

" I know but I doubt if he knows my new car. What about you?"

"My flat is pretty secure but I could go home for a while. Mum and Dad live in Wellington."

"Do it," Ellie advised. "Do you want the rest of the day off? I can ask your reliever to stay on with your class. Tomorrow too if you need it."

"No thanks. I need my class to take my mind off Jaxon. If I went home I'd just stew over everything."

SALEM'S COMMENTS PLAYED on Ellie's mind throughout the rest of the day. Sure, with the Japanese used import car that she purchased from her insurance money, Jaxon shouldn't know what she was driving. Of course all he had to do was to keep a discrete eye on the school carpark to see her drive out or even note what vehicle was parked in the principal's position. Of course, her grey Suzuki Swift was a popular brand and colour so would be hard to follow in busy city traffic.

She made a point of leaving school earlier than usual and at the gate, turned right towards the outer suburbs rather than the direct route downtown to her apartment. As well, she kept a constant look in the rear vision mirror but couldn't see his car. About two kilometres along suburban roads she drove back on the busy motorway, took the off ramp near the town centre and moments later entered her basement carpark. Everything appeared normal as she put the lift code in and arrived home safely.

Pleased but at the same time criticising herself for being paranoiac she relaxed and gazed out the window. Immediately below was the shop veranda roof so she couldn't see pedestrians beneath. However, the road itself was visible with late afternoon traffic moving slowly in both directions. The traffic lights turned red and the vehicles came to a stop. She almost turned away when something caught her eye. Behind a delivery truck was a car she immediately recognise. It was Jaxon's white Mazda CX5!

The lights turned green and she even recognised him wearing his inevitable baseball cap. Oh My God he must have followed her but how? She had driven in from the southern side of High Street as her apartment was on the east side of the road but he came along from the north. Perhaps he knew she had an apartment above the shops! There were not many of them so it wouldn't be hard for him to check them out. It was now about the time she'd normally get home from work so perhaps he had been parked a few blocks back and just waiting for her to drive past.

Her mobile rang. Frowning, she answered it after checking the number. It was unknown but certainly wasn't Jaxon.

"Ellie Parkes speaking," she said in her formal voice.

She recognised Salem's voice. "Are you still driving around or shopping?"

"No, I'm home. Why Salem?"

"Jaxon was watching from across the road from school when I drove out."

"In his car, a white Mazda."

"No. Just standing there. He looked angry, you know sort of hunched up with his cap yanked down over his eyes and his hands on his hips."

Ellie grimaced. Salem described Jaxon perfectly. You could just about tell his mood by the way he wore that damn cap.

"Can I come over for a wee while? Jaxon could come to my place?" Salem sounded nervous.

Ellie decided not to tell her that Jaxon had just driven by. "Sure. Drive down the ramp into the basement..." She gave Salem the code. "Park next to my car. I actually have two spaces allocated to me. See you soon."

After she clicked off she wondered if she should call Wyatt. He told her to do so any time and had given both his business and personal numbers. He had actually programmed them both into her mobile. She hesitated for a moment but it was after five so decided so she called him.

"Hi Ellie" said his welcoming voice. "I was just thinking about you."

She grinned for he must have programmed her name in his own mobile. "It's Jaxon," she said and explained everything that had happened to Salem and their latest worries.

"I'm in town at our Lower Hutt office. Would you like me to come around? I can be there in twenty minutes or so."

"It doesn't matter. Salem's pretty nervous so I asked her around. I just wanted to hear your voice."

"I'm coming!" He rang off.

Twenty-five minutes later Ellie heard a knock on the door. After glancing out the small window in the door she saw both Wyatt and Salem standing there. She grinned and opened it. Their company was just what she needed.

JAXON WAS FUMING AS he drove along High Street after parking at the northern end of the commercial area waiting for Ellie to drive by. Of course she could have gone to Queensgate Mall that had largely replaced the older shopping area that lined High Street. He had found out quite a bit about her and knew about her new car and that she was living in an apartment somewhere in the central city. He grimaced as he drove along by somewhat tatty shops now mainly occupied by second hand dealers and coffee bars. The larger firms had long gone to the mall, as had most of the banks.

From what he had learnt, many of the top floors had been converted to apartments that were popular with professional people rather than students. He stopped at lights and took a chance to gaze around. A sign caught his eye in front of a new five-storey block.

'Hillview Apartments, Stage 1 now completed,' the sign read. *'Only two apartments left for sale or rent to buy.'*

"My God, that's where she'd be," he muttered to himself. Ellie was a bit of a snob and wouldn't be interested in an old place. She'd want one of these new ones and no doubt her mother would help her financially. She had money to burn!

He continued onto a traffic island, drove around it and headed back up the street. After finding a spot to park he walked along to the building. It even had its own office in a modern shop off the footpath. He grinned for it was still open. He walked in to the smell of new paint. This is just what Ellie would be interested in!

An over-painted woman behind a counter greeted him with a smile.

"My neighbour said her sister had just moved into one of your new apartments and asked if I could drop off some books for her. However, I never got the number of her place. Could you help, please," he said.

"Of course Sir. And what is her name?"

"Ellie Parkes, I think."

The woman frowned as she stared at her computer. "I can't find her name here, Sir but we did have two families shift in this week. I believe one was a lady about your age."

"A blonde woman?"

She grimaced. "I think so, Sir. Sorry I can't help you more. Everyone else has left and I was just going to close up. Sally, our receptionist can help you tomorrow. "

"Can I stroll up and check?"

"Our security is pretty tight but what harm will it do?" She gave Jaxon a code for the lift, gave him other directions and smiled.

Stupid bitch should be fired for being so trusting. Mind you she had a good figure. It was a pity about the wedding ring on her finger, not that meant a lot these days.

Outside the lift was a list of tenants with six names and a column of blank parts, obviously apartments yet to be completed. One name caught his attention. *Annette Patterson Apartment 23.* My God, that would be her! Even had a surname starting with 'P' so she wouldn't forget it. That was typical Ellie who was always oh so precise.

He took the lift to the second floor, entered a posh looking foyer and found the apartment. He snapped several photos with his mobile and grinned. So far, so good!. He'd sort her out but had to be careful. It would be stupid to do something rash that led anything back to himself. An unfortunate accident should do the trick. A few days planning were worth the wait.

CHAPTER 6

When Jaxon planned his method of attack he decided to stay away from the school, as he was well known there. Also, without any knowledge of his movements his, oh so smart wife would grow complacent. As for Salem Milne, she was small fry and hardly worth any special effort. Women like her were plentiful and one would never know, down the track she might be worth hitching up with again. Jaxon grinned. Perhaps he could even practise his skill in persuasion if he talked to her at Ellie's funeral.

Also with Ellie gone, he would be financially better off, especially with that life insurance policy. No legal separation had come through as yet and he doubted if she'd bother to change her will that was one of those freebies that they had both made up not long after their marriage.

Over the following few days Jaxon discretely watched the apartment building. Yes every morning Ellie drove out in her small red car about quarter to eight and arrived home between five and six. It was funny though for he originally thought she had bought a grey coloured Suzuki but this was definitely her car. Though it was raining the following day he had glimpsed at her as she drove by. He saw her raincoat and blonde hair but other features were hazy in the rain. But that was her all right. She always wore that sexless old coat on wet days.

Other things about the building were interesting. Trade vehicles drove in and out all the time and workers in their yellow jackets were everywhere. There appeared to be no daytime security at all. Also the tenants appeared to be professionals, mainly women who drove out in the morning and returned at night. After a morning rush the vehicles and pedestrians at this end of High Street dropped away and by around eleven, the area was almost deserted.

Jaxon grinned. His original idea to vandalise her car was discarded. Even if he sabotaged the brakes for example, there was no way of making any resulting accident more than a minor inconvenience for her. He needed something that would kill her once and forever and appear to be an accident. Hiring a gunman to assassinate her like on those TV shows was just a fantasy and not realistic in real life. Anyway, if he did that it could easily be traced back to himself.

He'd concentrate on something in her apartment building but what? That was the question.

HAVING ACCESS TO THE apartment block in work hours was easy. By wearing a yellow safety jacket, helmet and a band of builder's tools around his waist Jaxon could go just about go anywhere. He noticed several points of interest. The new building appeared to be under construction in three stages, well four actually if one counted the shops on the ground floor that seemed to have a different firm building the interiors. The apartments in the four floors above ranged from completed ones where Ellie lived to partially built ones to the south and the higher floors. Just the framework was being completed on the top floor. A massive crane lifted components from street level to the site.

The middle section was the most interesting for sub-contractors such as electricians, plumbers and painters were everywhere. By discreetly talking to workers he found that there was an urgency to get the building completed. Apparently, the main contractor was several weeks behind schedule and many purchasers of pre-sold own-your-own apartments were complaining about being unable to shift into their unfinished apartments.

Jaxon grimaced. This would be Ellie! No doubt she conned her mother into financing her into buying rather than just renting an apartment. She was a spoilt little bitch who never thought of anyone except herself. He also noticed several contractors coming and going in the so-called finished apartments including the one Ellie obviously owned.

"They're having trouble with the pipes," one guy said to Jaxon. "There's natural gas for heating, hot water and cooking and electricity for air-conditioning with different contractors installing them. Damn stupid if you ask me. Natural gas is not as economical as it was so they should have just used electricity."

"So what's happening in the finished apartments?" Jaxon asked.

The man screwed his nose up. "There was a real stuff up. An inspector found the electric wires were too close to the gas pipes. They have to move the wires another thirty centimetres away from the gas," He laughed sarcastically. "As if that would make any difference if a gas leak blew up."

"Sounds typical," Jaxon replied, "Those bureaucrats are a pain in the butt."

The man nodded at him. "So you're not one of them?" he asked.

Jaxon laughed. "Me? No, I'm just one of those little guys one of the apartment owners called in to give a quote on an alteration. Wants an extra wardrobe built but the developers told them they'd have to pay for it themselves."

"Yeah. Sounds typical, I reckon the left hand doesn't know what the right one is doing around this place. Heard the developer is just about bankrupt. Anyway, see yah around."

The man gave a half wave and wandered off. Jaxon grinned as the information he had gathered made him begin to form a plan in his mind. Now what if....

JAXON CONSIDERED HIMSELF a bit of an expert when it came to explosives. After all, he had worked in a quarry in his younger days and had learnt about blowing up cliffside rocks in an opencast mine. Before he left he had nicked several timers that he had stored away years ago. It wasn't too difficult to buy explosive as farmers did all the time in rural areas. Just to be safe, he had set up a false bank account under an assumed name in a small town a hundred kilometres to the north.

They were more trusting in these places and it was dead easy to give a false rural delivery address. Purchasing explosive was no problem when he explained that he was a local farmer who was building a farm track through his farm and needed to blast through stony ground. Again this was quite plausible in the area.

However, the regulations had tightened over the last few years and he almost considered pulling out of the idea. It was a good one though, so he persevered and kept a record of everything he'd done, including the fake addresses and so forth. The guy serving him at the town's farmers' coop store where he went to buy the explosive was pretty casual. His own payments went though and soon he had enough explosive to wipe out the slut's apartment and make it appear to be a faulty gas explosion.

Luckily, the construction company building the block used several subcontractors for electrical work, plumbing, painting, laying carpets and so forth and there were also the government inspectors who checked everything. By reusing his tradesman disguise he was soon accepted as a legitimate visitor and even managed to get a security pass under an assumed name and company to attach to his work jacket. With often fifty or more workers on site during an ordinary working day there was nobody who knew everyone by sight or name.

As well as a basement car park, the building had a separate maintenance basement between the carpark and the ground level shops reached by pressing B2 in the lift. This floor had a low ceiling and actual natural lighting through horizontal windows at the back that were hardly noticed from an outside lawn area. Water and sewerage pipes ran the length of the floor. As well, the electricity, optic fibre, and natural gas pipes and wires went across the ceiling.

He could see the recent changes where pipes and wires had been shifted and there were many closed off pipes and dangling wires that he guessed would ultimately lead up to the unfinished floors above.

"Are you meant to be here, Mate? "

The voice made Jaxon jump in surprise. He spun around and saw a serious looking guy in the usual helmet and yellow jacket.

"Sorry, I've just been called in by one of the apartment owners who's having trouble with her hot water heating. I thought I'd come down here to see the source."

The man relaxed and grinned. "Yeah, we've had trouble as we had to shift some of the pipes. Bloody regulations, you know." He nodded over at a computer terminal. "Everything is centralised here. Hot water, you say?"

"Yes," Jaxon replied but when he told him Annette Paterson's apartment number he mistakenly used Ellie's first name. He gulped but the guy never made any comment.

He brought up a computer screen that showed the wiring and pipes of her apartment. He grimaced and pointed to the yellow lines onscreen. "It looks okay from this end. Mind you the apartments have internal instant water heaters for the showers and kitchen sink. If that's the case, the owner is responsible for any repairs. Mind you, it should come under the guarantee so she should contact the suppliers."

"That's me, I guess," Jaxon replied. "She's out working but told me to go straight in."

"Gave you her door code?"

"Yes," Jaxon lied.

The guy glanced at Jaxon's identity tag. "Okay but next time you should call us and don't just walk into this area."

"Sorry," Jaxon replied.

"No problem, Mate. Hope you can help her."

Jaxon walked out and took the lift to Annette's floor; he'd have to remember to use Ellie's new name, and went along to her apartment. Of course, the door was locked and used a remote to gain entry like those modern keyless cars. Now, he'd have to work out how to bypass the code. This however, proved to be impossible to achieve. Not even quite sophisticated methods he used on his mobile failed to open the door.

He sighed and glanced around the empty corridor. There were two lifts with one being a service elevator with a larger door and room inside to carry furniture, refrigerators and other bulky equipment. The rest of the corridor consisted of half a dozen apartment doors and a small room that was unlocked. Inside was cleaning equipment, vacuum cleaners and basic maintenance tools as well as a small bathroom for staff. This was adjacent to Annette's apartment.

Jaxon grimaced as a new plan began to emerge in his mind. Now if he...

ANNETTE PATTERSON LOVED her new apartment and considered that she was one of the lucky ones to be able to shift in on time. She worked in Wellington several kilometres down the motorway and was pretty busy in her position as a junior partner with a law firm. She had been recently promoted to this position and found the work quite demanding but more satisfying than being an employee assigned to mundane cases.

It was another wet and windy Tuesday morning when she drove out at her usual time. As she turned into the traffic in High Street she frowned for across the street a white car was parked with a guy just sitting inside. This in itself was not unusual but she had noticed it several times over the last week, always parked across the road and with the guy just sitting in it. What brought it to her attention though was in the evening the car was usually back again in more or less the same spot with the driver again sitting in it.

She shrugged as she drove by the car. It was probably some guy dropping his wife or partner off every day and picking her up at night. It was amazing how many modern women worked and their partners stayed home to look after the kids. There was probably a baby tucked away in the back seat. She grinned to herself and switched her thoughts to a recent client. The grizzled old farmer was having trouble with the Inland Revenue department and couldn't really understand why something he'd been claiming as a refund over the last thirty years had been refused in his latest return.

AT THOMAS ROAD SCHOOL, Ellie's life continued to be busy. There were always new issues with pupils, parents, teachers and the Board of Trustee members but overall everything ran relatively well after she had established herself as principal. Janice had adapted her methods to become more relaxed and both Salem and Karenza were conscientious teachers.

In her personal life, Ellie was becoming more and more attracted to Wyatt, if that could be called the word. She had to admit that there was more to it but Jaxon was always at the back of her mind. He was unpredictable and she had no doubt that he was planning something nasty.

But he hadn't!

Even Salem had heard nothing from him but he was still around town, she knew that much. He was not the sort to passively accept their separation and move on.

"I don't like it?" she said to Wyatt when he was around at her apartment one evening. "It's like the lull before an impending storm."

"You worry too much," Wyatt replied. "He's probably conning some rich widow at the moment, isn't that his style?"

Ellie laughed. "More probably shacking up with some nineteen year old university student whose parents are filthy rich."

"Oh the exciting life," Wyatt said and received a whack over the shoulder.

He grabbed Ellie's wrist and a moment later they were wrestling on the floor. It was gentle rather than violent, though and turned into a romantic frolic.

"By the way, haven't you got your school holidays again in a week or so?' Wyatt said after a gasping Ellie managed to squeeze out from under him and stand up.

She grinned. "For the kids, maybe but I've got plenty to do. The Ministry of Education wants us to reduce the size of our contributing zone."

"But why?"

"We're over-crowded and they don't want to build the two new classrooms we've been asking for. There is extra room at Redstone School only couple of kilometres away."

"So jack up that prefabricated classroom they've got and bring it to Thomas Road."

Ellie grimaced. "It doesn't work that way, I'm afraid."

"But you've still got time for a few days at the homestead? I'm taking a spot of leave and want to patch up that back porch. The Historic Places Trust has actually approved my latest plans as the back porch is out of of sight from the road and the new windows to close it in don't detract from the original design."

Ellie grinned. "And no doubt you have the windows already made and just waiting out there to be popped in."

"Well sort of. It costs a fortune in travelling costs to get a builder out there and the extra framework necessary isn't too hard to make."

"With me holding all the bits up."

Wyatt grinned and nodded. "It'll be a change from all the academic stuff you do every day."

CHAPTER 7

The noise or perhaps shaking must have awoken her. Ellie jerked awake to see an eerie red had replaced the normal darkness of her bedroom. Outside the top windows that she never pulled the curtains over she could see a sort of swirling red cloud. Next she heard a booming sound like thunder just down the street.

She switched the light on, jumped out of bed and rushed to her tiny balcony outside the living area. When she slid the door open she heard sirens and just stared. Further along High Street the new apartment complex was on fire. Flames were shooting high in the air and she could smell smoke. Fire engines howled past below her apartment and were followed by two police cars and an ambulance.

She slipped jeans and jacket on over her pyjamas, found her shoes and ran outside. Her immediate neighbours were all doing the same but nobody knew any more than herself. Together, they left their building to join a crowd that headed towards the burning building.

They were though, stopped by a hastily erected barrier between two police cars.

"Please keep back and unless you are a doctor or nurse, return to your homes," a police officer called though a loudhailer. "There was an explosion and there could possibly be more."

"What caused it?" A guy shouted from near Ellie but it was obvious the policeman never heard him above the roar of the burning building behind.

By now the fire brigade had connected their hoses and one ladder truck had backed in close to the building. Firefighters climbed it and aimed high-powered streams of water at the flames that had twisted up through three levels above with black smoke belching out everywhere. Other hoses were saturating the ground level floor and hoses led down to the basement.

Everyone around Ellie had an opinion about what caused the explosion and now raging fire but it was just that, people's opinion. The main action was to contain the fire and put it out, explanations about its cause would come later.

Two ambulances reversed up Hugh Street and through the barricades to where Ellie could see paramedics approaching with victims on trolleys. As far as she could see there were at least four people being loaded onto them

More sirens wailed as support fire engines, police cars and ambulances arrived. It appeared that the flames were being contained with the top floors now visible above the burning walls. The series of minor sounds of breaking glass and crumbling superstructure lessened.

"Just go home, folks," the loud hailer called out. "You cannot help and are hindering the way for emergency vehicles. Only the buildings immediately adjacent to the fire have been evacuated. If you live further away it is safe to return to your home."

THE QUITE LARGE CROWD, most in coats or jerseys pulled over night attire like Ellie's, turned and began to disperse. She had walked across the road to get a better view of the burning building so had to recross it to get home a couple of blocks away. As she zigzagged though emergency vehicles she noticed that towards home, the road was empty. A roadblock must have been set up back along High Street, probably at the traffic lights.

As she reached the far kerb, a hand seized her arm from behind. Annoyed, she swung around and found herself staring directly into a Jaxon's furious looking face.

"You bitch!" he snarled. "How did you get out?"

She gasped, yanked back and somehow managed to avoid being grabbed again.

"Just leave me alone, Jaxon. Go home!"

"Yeah, leave her Mate," a burly looking man in his mid-twenties towered over them both. "Is he bothering you, Lady?"

"Mind your own business," Jaxon spat but stepped away from Ellie.

She glanced at the guy and gave a whisk of a smile. "Thank you. He was annoying me."

"I'd leave the lady alone you pervert," the guy continued. "Piss off before I forget that I'm a gentleman."

Jaxon gulped and must have realised that he was no physical match for this stranger. He stared at Ellie. "It's all your fault," he muttered and slunk away.

"What does he mean?" the guy asked her.

"I've no idea," she replied. "I think he got me confused with someone else. Thanks again for your help."

"Need an escort home?"

"No thanks. I only live a few blocks away and there are people everywhere."

The last thing she wanted was for Jaxon to follow her home so she walked back across the road and turned up a side road, mixed in with a small group of pedestrians, circled around the block away from the burning building and checked to see if she was being followed. She couldn't see Jaxon but beyond the glare of streetlights and still burning building it was dark.

Moments later she was back home safe and secure. The experience though had been frightening and left her wondering about her ex-husband. Was it just a coincidence that he just happened to be there and what did he mean by his accusation?

She thought of calling or sending a text to Wyatt but stopped herself. It was now almost four in the morning and he'd be sound asleep. She now felt wide-awake so made a coffee and stared out the window. The streetlights had been turned off and the burning building was now covered in hazy smoke rather than flames. It appeared that the fire fighters had succeeded in containing the blaze.

With her mind churning over, she returned to bed and attempted to get a little sleep before morning arrived. It worked too for, moments later it seemed she awoke to find it was daylight with only the faint odour of smoke in the air.

DETECTIVE SERGEANT Layla Fraser stood in the basement of the building and stared around at three burnt-out vehicles, the now demolished lift and collapsed ceiling that appeared to be the epicentre of the explosion. Unfortunately there were two deceased victims who appeared to have been waiting for the lift when the explosion occurred.

"So it was an act of sabotage and not a natural gas explosion, Ralph?" she said to the explosive expert who accompanied her.

The elderly guy rubbed his chin and spoke with an English accent. "Aye it was. I've seen many of these in Northern Ireland when I was a young whippersnapper back before you were born, I'd say." Ralph raised an eyebrow. "By the way, congratulations on your promotion. You showed the guys up, I gather."

"Thanks Ralph," she replied.

"Aye, and how's the young guy going? Hardly out of high school, I'd say."

Layla laughed and turned to the detective constable standing a few metres away. "Meet Doctor Ralph Dalzel from the university. He's one of our top experts in explosives." She turned to Ralph. "This is Zach who has just come across from the uniform branch."

The pair shook hands. "You've got a good boss here, Zach," Roger said. "Stick with her and you'll learn a lot, I reckon."

"'I'm sure I will," Zach replied and glanced around. "So why would someone plant a bomb here?"

"Didn't know what he was doing. You know those sorts who know a little about things but think they know everything. He knew enough about explosions to cause all the harm but setting it off in the lift that I believed happened was a flaw in his planning."

"So what is your scenario, Ralph?" Layla asked.

"I think these two killed here were just in the wrong place at the wrong time. My examination of the floor above indicated that the assassin wanted to blow up one of the apartments on the floors above us. The guy and I'm assuming it was a man, did not take into account that someone would arrive and bring the lift down to the carpark. These modern lifts have time elements built in so even if he'd wedged the door open, after a few moments it would begin working again."

Layla nodded at the two unrecognised corpses lying on the floor beside a burnt out car. "Have these bodies been named?"

Ralph shook his head. "As you can see, it will take a forensic team to prove who they were. The CTV camera here was destroyed in the explosion but we can check the one at the main entrance to see what cars arrived before this all happened. I don't know what the guy's game was but the explosion was far too powerful to just wipe out a nearby apartment. Luckily, except for this basement and the two floors above, the full force exploded up the lift shaft and out the top, hence the spectacular flames that the locals saw. The actual apartments excluding those immediately above us received only superficial damage."

Layla nodded. "Yes, we checked the tenants out and will be having interviews with those involved. There were only these two deaths but several people have been hospitalised with burns."

"You can remove the corpses now," Ralph said. "We'll examine them more thoroughly in the morgue. Our main aim now is to find out their identity."

"We're onto that," Layla replied. "If they lived in the building it shouldn't be too hard to identify who they were."

ANNETTE AWOKE, FEELING numb down one side and glanced around at the unfamiliar scene. Everything smelt wrong and even the blankets were different. Someone was bending over her, a torch swished across her eyes and a warm facecloth dabbed her face.

"Hello, you're Annette Patterson I believe. There is nothing to worry about but you're in Hutt Hospital. I am Nurse Kathy Nansett..." The nurse held a tumbler up to her lips. "Just take a sip. Your throat will be quite raw."

"What happened?" Annette gasped after she swallowed some water and was helped up into a sitting position with the bed cranked up. Her throat was certainly sore and sort of throbbed.

"You were rescued from a fire in your apartment building," the nurse said. "I know it sounds silly but in some ways you were lucky that you were in bed and under your blankets. One side of your face and your right arm have second-degree burns that we are treating. Your arm is wrapped in a dry gauze and a special plaster covers your right cheek. Try not to touch it with your other hand." The nurse smiled at her. "Can you remember anything?"

Annette frowned as fragmented memories flashed back though her mind. There was a roar that must have awoken her, searing heat and the stench of flames. The entire wall on the corridor side of the bedroom had gone. Through this gaping hole, yellow and red flames roared by like one would see in a furnace. Her blankets were covered in soot, embers of wood and plaster.

She couldn't breath as she inhaled so yanked the blankets up over her face and found air beneath to breathe. Her whole face stung as did her right arm when she attempted to move it. Worse though, was the smoke that filled the air. Everything went woozy and the last thing she remembered was spluttering and gasping for breath.

"That's about it," she told Kathy. "I guess I passed out."

"The fire crew found you almost straight away and brought you here. You were not expected to awaken until mid-morning. It's now just after eight and about five hours after your rescue."

"Thank you," Annette said and felt her eyelids felt heavy.

The warm face cloth touched her face again. "Just relax," the nurse said. "You are quite heavily sedated but safe now. We will care for you."

THROUGHOUT THE DAY Annette awoke several times and had hazy recollections of doctors and nurses helping her. She had things explained to her and at one stage had a mug of warm soup. It was evening and dark outside when a nurse asked if she would talk to a couple of police officers.

"If you're not feeling up to it, I'll tell them to come back in the morning," she added.

"No, I'll talk to them."

A detective sergeant introduced herself and her companion as Layla and Zack. They listened as she repeated everything that she had remembered.

"Sorry, it is not a lot," she concluded.

"That's fine," Layla said. "We have just a few more questions for you."

Answering the questions, Annette stated that she had no known problems and her work companions were all likeable people.

"So you were recently promoted. Did that cause any resentment from other staff?" Zack asked.

Annette shook her head. "I don't think so. The other shortlisted candidates were all from outside the firm. Several of the staff congratulated me and joked about not having to whip a stranger into shape."

"They sound nice," Layla said. "Now a couple of personal questions. Remember we are not here to be judgemental but have you had any personal problems lately? You know, family problems, broken relationships and such like."

"No."

The questions continued until finally Layla concluded. "Has there been anything, no matter how unimportant it may seem that you noticed around your apartment or work place?"

"Not really," Annette replied. "Wait a minute; over the last couple of weeks there was a guy parked in a car across the road. He was there every morning when I drove out and still there when I arrived home in the evening."

"Every day?"

"Yes, even Saturday. I don't work in the weekend but there he was, just sitting in his car. He never returned in the afternoon."

"What sort of car was it?" Zack asked.

"A modern white one, a Mazda or Toyota I think."

"We'll check it out. Often these small items can be extremely helpful."

'Thanks," the sergeant said. "Later we'll need a more formal statement from you but there's nothing to worry about. Take care and we wish you a speedy recovery."

The pair shook her good hand and left. Annette frowned for she was curious. Perhaps that guy in the car was involved in some way!

TWO DAYS AFTER THE explosion, Ellie was at work in her office when Teresa on the front desk buzzed her. This was unusual for she usually just popped in if she wanted something.

"A Detective Sergeant Layla Fraser and wishes to speak to you," Teresa said.

"What about?" Usually if the police visited, it was something about school vandalism or something that pupils had done.

"She just stated it was a personal enquiry not associated with the school. Are you too busy to speak to her?"

Ellie frowned. Teresa was never usually this formal so probably the detective could hear everything she said. She grinned slightly. "I can give her a few minutes," she said when in reality she was just doing returns that were not urgent. However, with the police she was cautious especially if they arrived without warning and expected immediate access.

The detective who walked in though, looked pleasant and not in the least overbearing like her predecessor, a guy who had recently retired and had an abrupt manner on several occasions he had visited the school.

She extended her hand. "I am Layla Fraser, Mrs Parkes. I can come back at a more convenient time, if you wish."

"No. That's okay. Call me Ellie." She waved at one of the two armchairs beside a coffee table across the office. "Take a seat. How can I help you?"

She moved around and sat in the second armchair, which she did with most visitors. She had found this informal arrangement was more inviting than talking across her desk.

The detective smiled and opened a satchel she was carrying to bring out a photograph.

"Do you know this woman?" she asked and slid it across the table.

Ellie glanced at the photograph of a pleasant looking woman about her own age. She frowned. "Not in real life but isn't she one of the victims of that explosion on High Street? I saw this same photo on one of the TV reports."

"You are observant. Yes, this is Annette Patterson. She's still in hospital but should be released soon. We believe she is a victim that the arsonist was trying to kill."

"I see," Ellie said and fixed her eyes on the detective. "And why are you telling me this?"

"The information I am about to tell you is confidential. I am actually visiting you in an informal capacity and hope you will respect my request to keep anything you hear in that light."

"Sounds serious but I am at a loss as to why it involves me."

"Bear with me for a moment while I explain."

Ellie turned grim she tried to anticipate what the sergeant was about to tell her.

"So you've been checking on my background?" she almost hissed.

Layla nodded. "We believe you were the intended victim, not Annette."

"It's all about my former husband Jaxon, isn't it?"

"Who owns a white Mazda vehicle?"

"He does but go on."

"And you now live in an apartment in High Street two blocks away from the explosion?"

"Yes. I actually was awoken and went to see what was happening." Ellie clasped her hand across her mouth. "Oh hell!" she gasped.

"What is it?" Layla asked,

"When I was leaving the scene and heading home, Jaxon grabbed my arm." She explained what happened. "So you think he thought Annette's apartment was where I lived?"

"You are astute," Layla replied. "That's exactly what we believe. All evidence we have collected points to this fact. At a distance you are quite similar, same age and body size, even your hairstyle is similar and the business suit you're now wearing is not too different from what Annette wears. She's a lawyer in Wellington."

"But not close up! Jaxon would immediately know she wasn't me. Also mannerisms etcetera must be different."

"True but isn't he an extroverted guy who thinks knows everything?"

"That's him," Ellie muttered." He would often jump to a conclusion about some little thing and nothing I said would convince him he was wrong."

Layla took another photograph from her satchel and handed it to Ellie. The photo showed Jaxon sitting in his Mazda.

"Annette actually took this a week back. She said she was suspicious about the car but later convinced herself there was a harmless reason for him being there every day over the last couple of weeks."

"That's Jaxon, my husband."

Layla nodded

"She sounds a pleasant woman. Would it be possible for me to meet her or would that compromise your investigation?" Ellie continued.

Layla smiled. "That's what she asked. Before I visited here I told her that we suspected she was the victim of a mistaken identity. We even gave you a fictitious name of Chloe to make it easier to talk about how you may have been the real victim. However, all Annette knows is that you are a professional woman who lives near her apartment and a little information about Jaxon."

"I hope you have enough evidence to arrest him." Ellie retorted.

"We have but there is a second reason for my visit. He has disappeared and we have been unable to trace him. Can you help us find out where he might have gone?"

Ellie paled. "No," she whispered. "After leaving our marriage, I've been on a constant guard and have taken precautions to keep my apartment hidden from him. I have no idea where he could have gone." She grimaced. "Even when we were married he'd often have a 'lost weekend' as he called it but I knew it was an affair with some woman. I do have several names in my old diaries that could help, though I doubt it. He'd just move onto some other woman. That was what he was like, I'm afraid."

"Would you still like to meet Annette?"

Ellie nodded. "Yes. Somehow I feel responsible about what happened to her."

"You aren't," Layla replied. "I'll arrange it. I'm sure you'll like her. I meet all sorts of people in my profession and she is one that I believe is a genuine person." She smiled. "Not unlike you, I might add."

CHAPTER 8

It was funny how one's mental image of what to expect was completely different from real life. When Ellie stepped into the four-bed-alcove in the Hutt Hospital ward she was accompanied by Layla. She glanced around and noticed a woman on the far side wrapped in bandages and sort of propped up by the hoisted bed and pillows.

Beside the patient was another woman dressed in modern casual clothes who was helping to give her some food from a tray sitting on a frame across the bed. Ellie gulped but thoughts of sympathy largely dissolved when Layla addressed the woman helper, not the patient in the bed.

"Hi Annette," she said. "I hear you're going home today. This is Ellie that I told you about."

When the woman turned and smiled, Ellie noticed the scorched right side of her face and a bandaged arm.

"Hi Ellie," the woman said and extended her free hand. "Thank you for coming."

The handshake was firm and Annette's eyes warm.

"I needed to meet you," Ellie said. "I guess Layla told you about being mistaken for me. That photo you took of the man in the car was certainly my former husband, Jaxon. I wanted to apologise for everything that happened to you and your destroyed apartment."

"Why?" Annette replied. "You weren't responsible for what happened."

"Jaxon is a violent man and I was trying to keep away from him," Ellie muttered. "If I had not purposely avoided him he would not have mistaken you for me." She grimaced. "I live only two blocks along High Street from your place"

Annette nodded as she turned to fed the patient and talk gently to her. When a nurse arrived and offered to take over she walked across to another bed that had the blankets pulled back and a partly filled backpack sitting on it.

"I can leave at ten after one last check by the doctor," she said and again looked Ellie directly in her eyes. "I wanted to meet you, too."

After a little more casual talk that strangers participate in, Ellie was impressed by Annette .

"So where are you going when you leave here?" she asked.

"I've taken another week's leave from work and the company that owns my apartment have offered me a new one in the same building. It's another floor up and away from the damaged section. However, it won't be completed for another month or so. Between them and the insurance company they'll pay for me to stay at a motel over that time." She grimaced. "I'll need a new car, too. My old one was destroyed."

"I have a suggestion," Ellie said.

Annette raised her eyebrows.

"Come and stay with me. As long as you don't mind my ...err boyfriend. I guess you'd call Wyatt, popping in all the time, there's plenty of room. My spare bedroom is hardly used."

"But..."

"Well, come and see it and stay for a night or two before you make up your mind. I'm away all day and my apartment, like your old one, is close to everything. Motels can be so impersonal."

"That's kind of you. It sounds great."

Ellie glanced at her watch. It was a little after nine. "Send me a text after the hospital discharges you and I'll pick you up."

"Shouldn't you be at Thomas Road School? Layla said you were the principal there."

"The school won't fall apart if I'm absent for a couple of hours. It is more important for me to help you. It's the least I can do."

AS ELLIE TOLD WYATT a couple of days later, she guessed she had been feeling sorry for Annette when she invited her to stay. It had worked out well, though for Annette couldn't have fitted in so easily. Though she was obviously in some pain with mainly her burnt arm, she never complained. Luckily her face came off somewhat lightly with no actual scaring being present.

It was now the Monday evening a week later when Ellie arrived home just before six to see Annette's new car parked in the second parking allocated to her apartment. It was a black Suzuki Swift similar to her own one and had been covered by insurance. Wyatt had helped get her a good deal with the same firm where she had bought her replacement car.

Carrying two bags of groceries she took the lift up to her apartment and walked in to see that Annette had prepared a meal.

"Annette," she said. "I told you it wasn't necessary for you to cook a meal, especially since you are now back at work. I used to have mainly frozen meals during the week." She watched as Annett brought a large pie out of the oven. "Smells delicious."

She helped set the table and soon they were both sitting down enjoying a superb meal.

"So how was you first day back at work?" Ellie asked.

Annette sort of hesitated before she glanced up. "Everyone was great but tended to try to do everything for me rather than just letting me step back into my old routine. The younger ones seemed almost too embarrassed to talk to me."

"That just shows they care for you."

"Is my face too bad?" Annette asked.

"Of course not. It's like sunburn with the blister layer almost gone and replaced by healthy skin beneath."

"You're the true diplomat, aren't you?"

"Not really. That's the truth. How's the arm?"

Annette grimaced. "Okay, I guess but it aches if I try to do too much. The sling I thought would be unnecessary actually helps in the afternoon. I go back to the specialist on Wednesday to have that special bandage removed and hear what happens next."

"Do you want me to come with you?"

"No Ellie. You've done so much for me and Wyatt too, in talking that car guy down almost a thousand bucks so I never had to pay anything beyond the insurance payout. I ended up with a newer car with hardly any kilometres on the clock."

Ellie grinned. "He did the same for me. He's pretty well liked around town for being honest and helpful." She glanced at her companion who sort of played with her food. "There's something else, isn't there?"

Annette nodded. "I think I saw your ex outside our office. I am three floors up and have a view of the Lambton Quay. He was standing in the central part, you know where they have the gardens?"

Ellie nodded.

"He just stood there beneath one of those new trees they planted with his mobile held up as if he was taking photos. I could be wrong, of course for I haven't really seen him close up. His mannerism caught my attention, though. He was sort of slumped against the tree trunk almost like when he was in his car."

"Sounds like Jaxon," Ellie whispered. "Too lazy to even stand up straight. Did you contact, Layla?"

Annette shook her head.

Ellie took out her mobile. "So we'll do it, She said to contact her even if something didn't seem important. The news outlets have withheld your name but there were a couple of clips of yourself that I saw. If he had your name it wouldn't be too hard to trace where you work."

"But why me? "

"That's Jaxon," Ellie said. "In his warped mind he probably thinks you knew me before this all happened and we'd planned to trick him."

"But I know you now and am endangering you."

"So we tell Layla. Okay?"

She punched in the special number given to her and mere seconds later Layla was in video contact with them both.

"How's Ellie going, Annette?" Layla said with her eyes on her. "Giving you a stack of children's projects to mark?"

"No but I asked her to check out the books of an old farmer attempting to claim tax relief for a ute. He got grumpy when they turned him down."

The conversation changed to the reason for their call.

"That's interesting," Layla replied after listening to Annette. "We found his vehicle at the end of one of those roads up in the forest park. One can walk for weeks up there on those tracks. Some of the higher huts are hardly ever visited. We've been using drones to fly over them with high-powered cameras. Our new drones are pretty quiet and almost impossible to see from ground level."

"But no luck?" Ellie asked.

"Well we caught up with a couple of youths we're interested in and they're spending the night in our cells. Not Jaxon, I'm afraid."

"So it could be him in downtown Wellington?" Annette asked.

"Possibly. We'll have a look at the CCTV cameras in the central city at the time you mentioned. They're also pretty sophisticated." She turned to Ellie. "Do you have a recent photo of Jaxon, Ellie? If so, we can feed it into the CCTV and do a trace. Doing a broad search is too difficult as hundreds of sightings are often returned but a localised one could be successful.

"Sure. Give me a few moments and I'll get some back to you."

"Thanks. I'll keep in touch."

LAYLA AND ZACK ATTENDED the usual morning meeting to discuss new and ongoing cases called by Detective Inspector Caleb Stewart. The caseload was about normal with one quite violent crime from the night before taking up much of their time.

"And the Jaxon Parke's case, Caleb?" Layla asked near the end of the meeting. "That CCTV footage definitely showed him back in Lampton Quay near where Annette Patterson works."

The DI rubbed his chin as he gathered up documents on his desk. "We'll call off the search in the ranges and concentrate on this latest sighing. However, this latest case is your top priority at the moment."

"But why is Annette involved?" Layla persisted. "Haven't we established that she was a case of mistaken identity?"

"True," Caleb replied. "It appears that Parkes has now included Annette Patterson, in his revenge rampage. His personality refuses to accept that he is responsible for anything that goes wrong and transfers the blame to someone else, usually women. Medical experts report that this is not uncommon in cases like his." Stewart glanced up. "This case is getting to you isn't it Layla?"

"I think he is dangerous and we should step up trying to find him."

"Okay, you can follow up these sightings but your other case takes priority. Understood?"

"Yes Sir," she replied and caught her constable's eyes.

"You just have to know what buttons to push," she said to Zack as they walked out to their vehicle. "Caleb is a bit of a desk man but does listen to reasonable requests."

"Been around too long?" Zack asked.

"Possibly but I prefer him to some of the other senior officers we have," she added.

ELLIE GRINNED AT WYATT after their meal at a small local Indian restaurant that provided appetising meals that they both liked.

"So what do you want?" he asked.

"Is it so obvious?" she asked.

"Only when you think I might not agree but go on."

"When we visit the homestead over the weekend to get those back veranda windows put in, can I invite Annette, too?"

"Why? Doesn't she have her own friends to do things with?"

Ellie grimaced. "I don't think she has. Oh she has never said anything but I get the impression that she is, or was, totally devoted to her work at the expense of her private life. Her closest relatives live in Auckland where she has parents and a brother's family. She talks about a couple of nieces who are at high school up there and, in her own words, are at an age when they want to do their own thing."

"And she's also feeling self-conscious about her burns?"

Ellie nodded. "Luckily her face isn't too bad but her arm is a mess. She will need restorative skin graphs,"

"So you don't want her to stay at your place feeling sorry for herself?"

Ellie nodded. "She is pretty good at covering it but I know she gets down at times."

"And the other bit about Jaxon being seen near her workplace?"

"The police have confirmed that it was him but he has disappeared again. Mind you, I think Layla's trying to do all she can to help but her bosses are more concerned about that ongoing gang problem that erupted again last weekend."

Wyatt nodded. "Okay," he said.

"Okay what?"

"Ask Annette but don't be disappointed if she turns you down."

IT TOOK A LITTLE PERSUASION before Annette agreed to come with them to the homestead over the following weekend. During that time, no news had been heard of Jaxon. Layla had called in at school to report to Ellie that he was covering himself well, with no money withdrawn from his bank accounts and his mobile unused. There were no sightings by CCTV coverage of him anywhere in Wellington or Hutt City.

They were now on the road to the homestead just beyond where the seal ended and not far from where the bridge had been destroyed. Annette who sat in the back seat looked almost as excited as Cinders who gazed out the window with his tail wagging.

"I've never been out this way before," she said. "Prosperous looking country."

"Yes, mainly larger farms," Wyatt said. "Way back almost two hundred years ago my ancestors established the farm here. Only the homestead and a small piece of land remained when I inherited it. The rest is owned by an overseas syndicate."

"That won't work," Ellie interjected when she noticed Annette take out her mobile phone. "That last hill we came over cut out the signal."

Annette grinned, replaced it in her pocket and gave Cinders a pat. "He knows where we're going, doesn't he?"

"Oh yes," Wyatt laughed. "He loves the ocean and the hills."

They drove on until they came to the stream and bridge that still sat there looking grotesque like the back of a tip-truck tray above the tumbling stream. The other signs of the flood had largely disappeared.

"We have to ford the stream," Wyatt said. "The district council said they'll have a temporary bridge erected before next winter but we're pretty low priority, I guess."

He swung the Land Cruiser down a small concrete ramp, hit the water that splashed up to Cinder's delight and drove up the other side.

"The back of beyond," Wyatt replied.

"And so close to town," Annette replied.

"No disruptions either," Ellie said. "Nothing is worse than having a moaning parent call me over the weekend."

They drove on and a few moments later arrived at the homestead, all pristine with well-mown lawns but less cared for gardens.

"I pay one of the station workers to keep the lawns mowed," Wyatt said. "I admit that the gardens get away a little."

He pulled in beside the house and opened the door for Cinders who, with a woof, charged out and disappeared around the back of the house.

"He'll be back when he finds no food waiting for him on the back veranda," Ellie said

Annette climbed out and just stared at view of the ocean waves crashing on the beach way below them. "'Wow, a million dollar view," she said.

"Yes and without the tourists spoiling it," Wyatt replied. "Welcome to South Pacific View Station, Annette. Make yourself at home."

CHAPTER 9

Jaxon was pretty certain that nobody could trace the explosion back to him but one of his acquaintances, Leo, he couldn't really be called a friend, was on the phone disagreed.

"You're a silly bastard Parkes," he said. "If you wanted to do the old girl in, did you have to blow up half a building and then find out it was not her in the first place? You're in deep trouble, Mate"

"Why?" Jaxon felt his confidence plummet.

"This Annette Patterson survived but two others were killed when the lift exploded in the basement. The cops know far more than they're letting on in those public statements, you know. Buying explosives under an assumed name up in Levin was foolish as well. Everyone knows everyone in a place like that," Leo said

"How did you find that out?" Jaxon gasped.

"Does it matter? If I can, even the dumb cops will be onto you before long. I'm only telling you this because you helped me out last year."

Jaxon had helped Leo off a conviction at that time by providing him with a false alibi in a court case over a cache of drugs found in his car. Leo was a petty criminal and the cops moved on after the case collapsed.

"There's more," Leo said. "Apparently this Patterson woman was suspicious after seeing your car hanging around every day. She took a photo of you in your car and handed it onto the cops."

"How'd she get that? I never saw her around the car."

Leo laughed. "Oh don't be an idiot. You were looking out for the wife and not someone else. I guess she looks a bit like Ellie but not close up. You know great curves and upmarket clothes? She's a lawyer or something in Wellington."

"Damn!"

"Yeah, you've got a problem there, Mate. She survived the bomb and is now actually staying with Ellie in a flat two blocks away from the one you blew up."

"What!"

"You really stuffed that up, didn't you? I'd leave town for a while if I was you."

"Thanks Leo. That makes us even, I guess."

"Oh one more thing. Ellie's new boyfriend is Wyatt Sigley, you know that real estate firm here in town. It seems he owns some flash place down over on the other coast. His parents were filthy rich and owned the South Pacific View Station. Heard of it?"

"No."

"Yeah well, it was in his family for several generations and was sold off to a Chinese syndicate a decade or so back. He still owns the old homestead, though, so must be rolling in cash."

"The bitch!" Jaxon snarled.

"Yeah, she landed on her feet. My advice is to forget about her and move on."

"Are you kidding? She owes me, you know."

"Suit yourself, Mate. But now you've got two of them onto you. When a woman gets her fangs into someone you're doomed and now there's two of them. Lie low and take care for a while. I'm sure it'll all blow over. I heard that the pair that were killed in that explosion were married."

"So the cops think they were the intended victims?"

"Could be but it's all rumours. If I find out more I'll get back to yah."

AFTER THE CALL, JAXON had plenty to think about. It didn't sound too bad but this Annette could be a problem now she had met up with Ellie. If he could dispose of both of them his problems would be over.

That news about that place Wyatt Sigley owned was interesting too. Perhaps he could leave town for a while and go and visit the area. There were bush areas around with huts on the walking trails and perhaps beach cottages. He didn't like tramping or country life but in the short term, Leo's idea of lying low for a while was a good one. It was a bit like killing two birds with one stone, so to speak.

JAXON WAS QUITE PLEASED with himself. By accessing Ellie's savings account online he withdrew twenty thousand dollars that he deposited into his new account with a different bank under the assumed name he had used when purchasing that explosive in Levin. With this money he bought a pretty good Toyota camper van. He got a good deal from the American tourists who were returning home after spending several months touring New Zealand. It lacked the power of his Mazda but it would be inconspicuous in the back blocks. He had thought of just stealing a car but decided that if he wanted to disappear for a while a stolen vehicle could be traced too easily. Also Ellie had the money so why not use it?

He chuckled. It'd all end up his after she was disposed of anyway.

Next he bought outdoor gear and food for several weeks. Also there was his old hunting rifle he had owned for years with enough ammo stored so he didn't need to buy more. He also hitched his old motorbike on the back of the camper van for it could come in handy. Finally he headed out to that God forsaken beach that the South Pacific Station was near. He'd survey the area and with a little luck, Ellie would come out to the homestead one weekend. She liked getting out of town and now with this new guy this was a perfect place to go.

If not, he'd return back and solve the problem and with that other bitch, too. Afterwards he could just head down south or perhaps even Australia for a new life.

IT TOOK LONGER THAN expected but after fording the river where a bridge had collapsed, Jaxon drove on a few kilometres before there on the right was the homestead. It appeared to be in a reasonable state with the lawns around recently mowed and a hedge along one side trimmed but the gardens were uncared for so the place had that empty look.

Ready with an excuse about being a tradesman if he met anyone, he drove in and followed the drive around the side of the main building, Here, he was out of sight from the main road so locals driving by wouldn't see the van. He climbed out and glanced around. The place was empty with no sign of anybody being there.

He strolled around but there seemed to be no security cameras so he tried a back door. It was locked as expected but with an old fashioned lock that took mere seconds to bypass. Inside, everything was quiet with that slightly musty smell of being closed up for quite a while. The electricity was unexpectedly still on and the nearby deep freezer was the probable reason for this. He opened it to find frozen food including basic stuff and several packs of frozen meat.

He spent an hour or more examining the house and surrounding grounds. There was a large impliment shed with modern vehicle doors installed in the building that looked as old as the homestead itself. Apart from the weedy garden, the place was in good condition and had been well maintained. Around the back a long veranda had several glass windows leaning on the wall. They were these pre-made ones that would be attached to waist high balcony along the veranda.

So someone would be returning to do this? With a little luck it could be Ellie and this Sigley guy. He grimaced at the thought of his wife in bed with someone else. No wonder he had gone off the promiscuous bitch. She's probably been screwing other guys for years.

After considering whether to stay here he decided it wasn't worth the risk so drove out and travelled the quite short distance back to the beach. It was in a bay flanked by cliffs on the northern end. About a dozen beach cottages along the beach all appeared empty and awaiting their owners in the summer. At the far end of the tiny village was a small campsite with a facilities block that was unlocked. A noticed from the local district council welcomed visitors and asked that the facilities be left in good condition and all rubbish be removed when one left. There was a water supply and coin operated power supply, a kitchen sink, stove and two tables. Outside, an adjacent toilet block appeared clean and included showers. The district council obviously maintained it well, even in the off-season.

There appeared to be nobody around but a log-book in the kitchen showed that several people had stayed there over the off-season. Jaxon grinned. This was a perfect place to stay.

He picked a site behind the buildings to park the van and was pleased he had brought his motorbike with him. It would be handy to use to keep on eye on the homestead and to also see what else was around.

He was annoyed to find there was no mobile contact. His iPad like the mobile had no coverage. There were no FM radio stations available but the AM stations from Wellington included a talkback station. The non-commercial public radio also had good news coverage. There was no TV but who needed it anyway?

He grinned as the news about the explosion and apartment fire was superseded by other local news. There was always crime, accidents and doom to satisfy listeners. Mind you, those on the national radio were a pompous lot that he never listened to at home.

THE FOLLOWING MORNING that was a Thursday, not that the day made much difference, Jaxon returned to the homestead on his motorbike to have a real look around. As expected, he was alone and this was almost frightening. All his life he had people around him and the sheer loneliness of being in this isolated area sent shivers up his back.

The search of the house revealed nothing unexpected. It appeared that this Sigley guy only used a small living area with an adjacent couple of bedrooms and bathroom to live in on his visits. The grand looking living areas at the front had sheets over furniture and smelt stuffy and were dim from closed curtains. Upstairs areas consisted of unused bedrooms, bathrooms and an alternative living area.

There was no sign of Ellie having been there but the main bedroom contained women's clothes and a photograph of a woman about his age. There appeared to be no other personal items though several drawers contained documents that were a decade or older and were of no interest to him. Other items in the living area contained the usual household items. Only the kitchen contained a modern microwave.

Jaxon never moved anything and was careful to leave no trace of his visit. He continued exploring the grounds. The impliment shed contained a modern ride-on lawnmower and there was also a utility vehicle with an attached trailer. A chainsaw and other gardening equipment, bags of fertiliser and garden stuff were also packed neatly on shelves. The garage part contained a vintage vehicle that looked as though it was being renovated.

He noted that the paddock grass outside was short and sheep wandered around. Several gates were open to allow them access to other paddocks. Probably, these belonged to the new owners of the South Pacific View Station. He knew there were houses in a cluster up the road across the river where the manager and workers on the station lived.

He looked up at a nearby hill that was forested near the top. He squinted and noticed a small building near the peak of the closest hill. Could this be a forest hut built to accommodate trampers and hunters? It appeared too large to be just a pump shed that many local farms had. Anyone who was up there he could easily see the homestead below.

After lunch back at the camping ground, he studied a quite modern topographical map he had brought with him. Yes, the walking and cycling tracks showed with a code for their difficulty and where huts were. The hut he was interested in was named McArthur's Hut. It was small but provided bunk and facilities for six and was two hours walk from the camping ground. He couldn't be bothered walking for that time but he could ride his motorbike there. He packed a small overnight bag and food just in case it was worth staying overnight in the hut and headed out on the motorbike.

Ignoring a sign that said the track was only for walking or cycling he roared along. If it was built for cyclists as well as pedestrians he guessed there would be no steps to hinder his progress. He was right for although some sections were steep, his trusty old motorbike coped well and half an hour later he arrived at McArthur's Hutt to find it empty. Inside were the usual facilities and a logbook that had been most recently filled in by trampers a month earlier.

Using binoculars he had brought with him he focused on the homestead way below. There was someone there! He muttered but relaxed when he saw a woman mowing the lawn. Now, that was a good sign for perhaps Sigley was going to visit over the weekend. With a little luck, Ellie would be with him.

Another advantage of the hut was that his mobile was in range. After reading his messages that told him little, he made a call to Leo.

"I've been trying to get to you, Mate," Leo's voice boomed out through the speaker. "Where are you?"

"At a hut in the hills," Jaxon replied but didn't elaborate.

"Well take my advice and stay there for a while," Leo replied. "It's all turning to crap back in town."

"How?'"

"The cops want you and have plastered your face all over the TV and newspapers. I reckon you must he at the top of their most wanted list at the moment."

Jaxon fumed. "Have they talked to you?"

"Me? No Mate but plenty of the other guys you know have been visited. Tarts too. They all sound as mad as hell. One of them came from Ellie's school. Isn't that a bit close to home?"

Jaxon's mind turned to Salem Milne. He guessed he should never have had an affair with her. Perhaps that was just to get even with Ellie for Salem was hopeless in bed and a bit of a snob.

"Have you still got contacts with those passport counterfeiters? I need one under an assumed name to get out of the country," he continued.

Leo hesitated. "It'll cost you Mate, even more now that your face is plastered everywhere. I don't like dealing with them, either. These big time international syndicates don't like being crossed, you know."

"Okay, forget about then," Jaxon spat.

"I can get you another fake driver's licence but that's about it," Leo muttered.

"Don't worry, the one I have seems to be holding out."

"It's up to you, Mate. If you want any supplies, I can meet you somewhere."

"Could need some in a few days. I'll get back to you. Has Ellie been on TV?"

"Nope. She's keeping a low profile, I reckon. I know the cops have visited her at that school where she's the boss but that's not unexpected. I'll keep in touch!"

Jaxon clicked off and grimaced. Just when he thought everything was slipping into place, all hell breaks loose again. If his ex had been a bit less of a know-it-all, things would have been different. It was all her fault. Damn her!

He glanced at his watch and decided that he might as well stay in the hut for the night. He had brought enough food for a couple of meals and he'd noticed a few cans of stuff in the hut cupboard. At a pinch he could stay here over the weekend. Perhaps he should light the fire for once evening came it could get damned cold up here.

Luckily, there was plenty of firewood all split and ready to use and a kerosene lantern with a three-litre can of fuel almost full to top it up. He walked out and used his binoculars to study the homestead below. The woman mowing the lawns had gone and the place appeared empty. He swung his binoculars around but could see nothing except the empty road and part of the beach. The few beach cottages and his van were out of sight.

Clouds had built up over the ocean and were coming in from the southeast. This also indicated that the weather could turn colder. Of course this could be good for trampers and hunters would stay away.

FRIDAY ARRIVED WITH the weather clearer but the clouds still hung around. He'd had a lousy night but by morning he was more or less ready for another day. It was chilly so he stoked up the embers in the fireplace, added wood and soon had a fire going. After breakfast and a can of beer he felt better and wondered outside. There was a mist over the ocean but he could still see the homestead. Everything around looked empty and forlorn.

He decided though, to stay at the hut for another day. At least he was in mobile range here and could maintain contact with the world below. He spent half an hour splitting wood. It was dry, the axe sharp and the effort wasn't too strenuous. The pile he made more than replaced the wood he had used in the fire. He grinned and wondered what Ellie would say about his achievement. Damn it, why did he always have her enter his mind about things?

He shrugged, found that the fire must have a wetback to heat water for the shower was warm. A relaxing shower was what he needed. However, by two in the afternoon he was totally bored and considered going back to the camper van.

The mist had cleared and he sat on an outside bench when he heard distant voices. Three people appeared along the trail on the uphill side. Two were women, they all looked young and by the way they walked, somewhat exhausted. The nearest hut in the direction they came from was a four-hour walk away so they must have set out early.

The guy in front of the line gave him a wave as they approached. Jaxon stood and waited with mixed thoughts. In some ways their arrival was a damn nuisance but on second thoughts if they were in the forest they wouldn't have seen his photos on the news. He grinned and stepped forward to meet the strangers.

CHAPTER 10

Scarlett Evans glanced at her companions around her and grimaced. There were three in their tramping party, all second year Victoria University of Wellington friends who flatted together in a small inner city apartment. The guy with them, Karson looked as tired as she felt but her friend Narla still seemed to be able to bounce along at almost a trot.

This was their third day of a planned five-day tramp through the remote Aorangi Forest Park and they were approaching their third hut after a somewhat gruelling five-hour tramp. Like the other Department of Conservation huts, this would have six bunks and other amenities. When it came into view her relief was partly restrained by the smoke coming from the hut chimney.

Damn, someone was there!

She glanced past Karson who was in the lead and noticed a guy get up from where he was sitting on a deckchair and almost glower at them before acknowledging Karson's wave as he stepped forward.

To Scarlett he looked anything but a tramper with a can of beer in his hand, bit of a potbelly and unshaven face. Most guys had a beard or whatever now-a-days but he just looked unkempt. Next she spotted a motorbike parked against the hut. So he wasn't a tramper! Narla shrugged and grinned at her.

Unlike with other trampers they'd meet at the last hut, she was glad they had Karson with Narla and herself.

When they met and shook hands the guy said. "Name's Wayne. Come down from Woolstone Hut? Quite a walk, I hear."

"About five hours," Karson said after they introduced themselves. He nodded at the motorbike. "I see you're not a tramper."

"Yeah well, I'm from DOC and doing a routine inspection to see what repairs and so forth are needed at this hut. A motorbike is cheaper than using a helicopter that we use for the top huts."

"So you aren't staying?" Narla asked. She always said what she thought.

The guy grinned. "Sorry but there's only me. You three can use the bunkroom and I'll crash on a mattress in the living area, tonight. I'll be recommending new mattresses in my report. After a few years these old ones need replacing." He glanced back at the hut. "Otherwise, for its age the hut is in quite good condition. There are no roof leaks and the water system is sound. Anyway, come in. I've had the fire going so there is hot water if any of you want a shower."

His eyes caught Scarlett's and seemed to stare at her whole body. She felt unnerved and remembered what her over-protective mother told her when she first left home. That was to always stay in a group if she was away from the apartment overnight. To her at the time, this was just Mum being fussy but on a few occasions over the last couple of years she had followed this advice.

Perhaps she was wrong. This Wayne guy seemed okay during the rest of the afternoon and spent time splitting more firewood and studying the valley below through binoculars. There was a lovely view with waves rolling into a bay. There was a flat area of paddocks while to the left were the only buildings in view.

Wayne ambled over to her and nodded at the view. "There's a small village just beyond the sandhill to your right with a camping ground and handful of beach cottages. That house you can see in the other direction is the original homestead of the station."

"Station?" Scarlett queried.

Wayne grinned. "That's what they call large farms mainly here and in the South Island. The homestead you can see is still owned by the ancestors of the original settlers but a Chinese syndicate owns the station itself. There are three newer houses and farm buildings where the manager and workers live. They're also out of sight behind the hill. Like a look through my binoculars?"

"Thanks," Scarlett replied and accepted the binoculars to look at the view."

"So the old homestead is empty?" she asked after focusing on it.

"Yeah. A real estate guy inherited it. I think he plans to do it up and sell it. He visits once in a while."

"Looks lonely," Scarlett said. "So there are hardly any permanent residents in the area?"

"Nope. just the South Pacific View Station manager and possibly one other family. The place livens up in summer but is still away from the popular beaches further north at Riversdale and Castlepoint. " He shrugged. "The road in is rough and hilly. City types can't be bothered with the gravel road."

He ambled away and Narla joined her. "You were talking a lot to that creepy guy, weren't you?"

Scarlet nodded. "Oh he's not too bad. Told me a bit about the history of the area." She repeated what Wayne had told her.

"I still say he's a creep and doubt his story about being employed by DOC. Wouldn't he have at least be wearing an official jacket or have some sort of identification?"

Scarlett laughed. "God, you sound like my ultra-cautious mother."

"Okay," Narla replied. "I like your Mum though. She's done more for me than my own parents over the last year or so."

"Yes, Mum's fine but can still be a pain in the butt at times."

They were interrupted by a shout from the hut door.

"Hey you two, want an afternoon coffee?" Karson called. "The kettle's boiling."

BY FIVE, MASSIVE BLACK clouds had moved in from the ocean and over McArthur's Hut. Huge drops landed and seconds later a torrential downpour lashed the tiny building. Fork lightning lit up the sky before thunder roared.

"We should be okay," Karson said as he peered out beyond the veranda where the spouting couldn't cope and water streamed down from the roof like a waterfall.

Scarlet stared at Narla. The storm was frightening but at least they comparatively safe in the hut. If it had arrived a few hours earlier they'd have been caught in the full blast on the higher slope.

They all cooked up a good meal with even Wayne helping. Afterwards, everyone seemed to want to just ignore the storm and relax. Scarlet found some decade old magazines to flip through while the two men started a card game.

It was a game Scarlet vaguely remembered so she watched them play. This Wayne seemed quite an expert and grinned whenever he won. However, Karson appeared to be learning the tricks of the game and soon began to catch up. When this happened, Wayne's face dropped and at times he challenged cards Karson played. His attitude appeared to reinforce Scarlet's original dislike of the man.

She stood up and said she'd boil the kettle and make everyone a drink. She glanced around to see that Narla wasn't in the room. She walked through to the bunkroom to see her lying on a bunk studying her mobile.

"Are we in range?' she asked.

Narla looked glum. "Yeah but I'm low on power so didn't turned it on until a few minutes ago"

"So what's the problem?" Scarlet said as she sat on the edge of Narla's bunk.

"This!" Narla whispered and turned her screen for Scarlet to see.

Scarlet frowned for there was a photo of Wayne filling the page. Beneath was a headline, *If anyone knows the whereabouts of Jaxon Parkes, please contact the police.*

Beneath the smaller print told little except that he was wanted by the police. The news site believed it was related to the recent explosion in a new apartment complex in Hutt City with two fatalities and several injuries by residents.

"It's him," Narla gasped. "I wondered about his name. He didn't just automatically reply the few times I called him Wayne."

Scarlet stared at the photo. "So what do we do?" she asked.

Narla pointed at the text. "We should call the police. There's a special number to use."

"Ask Karlos first. He needs to know." Scarlet stuck her head out the door. "Karson, can you come and give us a hand with the mattresses on the top bunks?"

When Karson glanced up, she glowered and signalled to him with a finger. He in turn frowned but placed his cards down. "Won't be a minute..."

Ignoring Wayne's mutter, he came across to the bunkroom. Scarlet shut the door and held Narla's mobile out.

"Have a look! It must be him!"

Karson studied the photo and read the text.

"I reckon we should call that number before my battery runs out," Narla turned to Scarlet. "Can you do it? You're better at explaining things than me,"

"Sure," Scarlet replied and punched in the number.

THERE WAS AN ALMOST immediate reply. "Detective Sergeant Layla Fraser speaking. You have reached a police enquiry number. How can I help?"

Scarlet nodded at the others two and explained about themselves, where they were and why she was calling.

"We are not completely certain but think that this man here at the hut with us is the Jaxon Parkes you wish to find," she concluded.

"And this McArthur's Hut looks down on the coast below?" Layla asked.

"Normally it has a good view but we're in the middle of a thunderstorm at the moment and can't see much out there."

"I've got a Google satellite view of your area on my other screen. It appears you would normally see the old South Pacific View Homestead below you. Is that correct?"

"Yes but there's nobody there."

"Have you looked lately?"

"No, Not with this storm. I can send one of my friends out to have a look."

"That can wait. Just be extremely careful. Jaxon Parkes is an unstable and possibly violent man. Does he know you're using a mobile?"

"No we're in the bunk room with the door shut."

"That's good thinking. Don't even give him a hint that you know who he really is. Can you all do that?"

Layla continued with more advice and said that the police would arrive as soon as possible but this could be quite a while due to the storm and distance. "Remember, don't aggravate or change your behaviour towards him. If you suddenly become too friendly for example, he could become suspicious. Also don't suddenly change your plans or try to leave. Okay?"

"Is that homestead important?" Narla who overheard the conversation, asked.

"Yes. We believe his estranged wife Ellie may be visiting there over the weekend and could be in danger. The homestead down there is out of mobile range. I'll get a police party to head out there pronto.

After a few more instructions and thank you, the detective gave Scarlet codes to use if Jaxon became hostile. Also there was a new personal number to use if immediate contact was required.

Scarlet disconnected and handed the mobile back to Narla.

"It sounds grim," Karson said, "but you did so well. I doubt if I could have been so calm."

Narla caught his eyes and nodded.

THE MEN CONTINUED TO play cards for almost an hour. Wayne that they now knew was really called Jaxon finally won by a small margin. They all had a cup of coffee before they said night to Wayne and retired to the bunkroom. By now the storm had stopped but a wind had risen and rattled the doors and windows.

"Us girls will take the top bunks at the far end," Narla said. "Just in case the creep gets fancy ideas."

"Why not?" Karson replied. "Though I doubt he'll try anything. It's lucky you two weren't tramping alone though."

Scarlet grinned at him, "And I thought you'd be my main problem on this trip."

"And be lashed by your mother's tongue when we got back?"

"Oh come on!" Scarlet replied with a grin. "We got over that row when I told her at the beginning of the year that I was going into a mixed flat"

SCARLET AWOKE TO FIND it was still dark but she needed to go to the toilet. The hut had one next to the shower in a small bathroom adjacent to the bunkroom. To access it she would have to go through the living area where Wayne had bunked down on the couch.

"I need to go, too," said Narla in the darkness. "We could go together."

Feeling around for the darkness was total and she didn't wish to turn her torch on, Scarlet reached out, grabbed Narla's hand and together they pushed the door open.

A light was moving around across the room. Jaxon must be awake and moving around.

"He's outside," Narla whispered and practically dragged Scarlet across the room to the bathroom.

Once there, Scarlett turned her torch on and sighed in relief. There was a latch on the door that she slid across. After they both used the toilet they now had to get back,

Again she turned the torch off and pushed the door open. Light reflected from the opened outside door where Jaxon still was.

"Come on," Narla said, "It's only a few metres."

They had almost reached the bunkroom door when the full beam of Jaxon's torch caught them.

"So you have returned, Ellie?" the angry man roared. "I'll show that you can't just walk away from our marriage whenever you feel like it."

He stepped forward and seized Scarlett by the arm, twisted it up her back and gave her an almighty shove. She screamed as she hit the wall and landed on her knees. She turned, just as a boot hit her in the shoulder. She rolled sideways and in those few seconds noticed the torch beam cutting across the room.

Narla screamed and jumped on Jaxon's back and began bashing him with her hands.

"Bitch," Jaxon howled and turned to fend himself off Nellie, who though twenty kilograms lighter than the guy managed to scratch him across the neck with her fingernails.

Scarlet scrambled to her feet but was hesitant about what she should do. Jaxon, though, flung Narla aside and turned back towards her. She covered her face with her arms and attempted to fend off the attack.

But it never came!

A torch blazed out for Karson had arrived. Jaxon was grabbed and flung back across the room. He staggered to his feet but cowered back, now the victim not the aggressor.

"It's all a mistake, " he whimpered. "I thought she was Ellie, my wife."

"So you attack your wife on a regular basis, do you?" Karson retorted as he grabbed Jaxon's shoulders. He looked as if he was going to punch him with a closed fist when Scarlet grabbed his arm.

"Don't Karson!" she cried. "He's not worth it!"

The situation was tense.

Karson relented but held Jaxon at an arm's length. "Your welcome here has expired, Wayne or whatever your real name is."

Scarlet felt relieved that Karson never revealed that they possibly knew his real name was Jaxon. That would have made matters worse!

Karson still had Jaxon in an iron grip but turned to her. "Did he hurt you, Scarlet?" he asked.

"He would have!" screamed Narla. "He kicked her and would have done more if I hadn't tried to stop him."

"And you did," Scarlet added. "Thank you.'

"Did you now?" Karson pulled the terrified-looking Jaxon in until he was mere centimetres from his face, seized him around the throat and just about throttled him. The man was actually gurgling and turning almost blue when Karson finally relaxed his hold.

"Don't!" Scarlet again attempted to calm Karson down. "He's had enough!"

"Like all bullies, you don't like being on the receiving end. It's lucky for you, Scarlet doesn't even like seeing scum like yourself hurt."

"Name's Jaxon." He caught Scarlet's eyes. "Sorry, you looked like Ellie in the dark."

"And I imagine that she is a lovely lady," Scarlet whispered and returned his stare until he looked away. "Just get your gear and go!"

She turned and almost ran back into the bunkroom as tears rolled down her cheeks.

SCARLET LIT THE KEROSENE lantern and the glow was helpful in lessening the situation with Jaxon now sitting in an armchair.

"I am not interested in your family life, Mate," Karson said in a quiet voice. "If you think it is normal to turn to violence to solve your problems though, my advice is to seek help." He glanced at his watch. "It will be dawn in about forty minutes. You can get dressed, have a shower and breakfast then just leave on your motorbike. If you're was still at that camping ground by the time we arrived down there, you will regret staying around." He squeezed Jaxon's chin and just stared at him.

"I'd listen to him if I was you," Narla added. "The last guy who crossed Karson ended up in hospital with a broken jaw."

Karson hid a grin. He'd never actually been in a fight since high school days but worked out at the gym regularly. By the look of Jaxon's quivering lips, the guy believed her story.

"I'll get my gear packed," he muttered. "I doubt if my wife is in the area anyway. She doesn't like the back-blocks."

Forty-five minutes later Karson heard the motorbike start and watched as Jaxon headed out without even a backward glance. The sun had risen over the horizon to the east and the storm of the night before had moved on. With a little luck they wouldn't see him again.

SCARLET AND HER FRIENDS tidied the hut, and made an entry in the hut's log-book. This included just a brief note about Wayne, the name they used to fit in with a brief entry he had made when he arrived.

Scarlet turned to the others, as they were packing.

"I think we should change our plan to continue to that last hut on our itinerary," she said.

Karson grinned. "So you saw that there were people at that homestead below and think they could be in danger?"

"But how will we get home?" Narla asked. "We arranged for your mum to pick us up the day after tomorrow at the road-end close that other hut."

"So we call her and just say we changed our minds and changed the pick up point." Scarlet frowned. "We won't tell her about Jaxon though. You all know how she worries?"

Karson nodded. "Just say we decided to stay at that camping ground at the beach for our last night due to the stormy weather."

The others agreed so with everything arranged including a report about Jaxon to the police, they headed out half an hour later. Scarlet could make out a Land Cruiser at the homestead just before everything below disappeared from view as more storm clouds rolled in. Also, as expected their mobiles lost contact.

For better or worse, they were now on their own.

CHAPTER 11

"Well, half done," Wyatt said as he wiped his brow and admired the two new windows installed along the homestead's back veranda. "Just before that next storm arrives."

It was close to ten in the morning on Saturday and they'd been working on the installation since breakfast.

"Yeah!" Ellie gasped. "We did all the holding while you just screwed it all in."

"I didn't mind but just having one hand to use didn't help." Annette added.

The veranda being enclosed was on a rear corner with the two new windows placed on the west side above the original waist high wall. When the end two south facing windows were installed, the veranda would become a conservatory to relax in.

"So how is it you can alter this?" Annette continued. "Didn't you tell me the Historic Places Trust won't let you alter the exterior?"

"It's just their stupid regulations. As long as this rear of the homestead can't be seen from the front we can change it. My dad had to originally leave that top chimney in for it could be seen from the road. Another chimney down the back and out of sight was ripped out years ago when the laundry was upgraded." Wyatt grinned. "But let's stop for now. The rain will be coming full blast in from the south soon."

Cinders, who was sitting nearby stood up, crossed to the new window and growled.

"What is it Boy?" Wyatt strolled along and looked out the same window.

"Okay what's wrong?" Ellie asked.

"Oh nothing really. There are three trampers on the back track. I guess we'd better offer them shelter from the storm."

Ellie followed his gaze and saw a line of three moving through the back paddock.

"There's a designated track there that's a spur from the main one coming down from McArthur's Hut to the beach. Most trampers go the other way," Wyatt explained.

Five minutes later the trampers arrived through a back gate. The woman who approached them smiled almost shyly and held out her hand to Ellie who had stepped forward.

"I'm Scarlett Evans," she said "Are you Ellie Parkes?"

Ellie frowned as she shook the woman's hand. "I am actually but how did you know me? I don't think we've met before."

"So you're okay?" Scarlett gasped. "We were worried about you."

"And why is that?" Wyatt cut in.

"When we arrived at McArthur's hut yesterday this guy was there..."

Scarlett briefly told them about meeting Jaxon at the hut.

"The last we saw of him was when he roared away on his motorbike early this morning," Karson concluded. "We contacted Detective Layla Fraser and she said the police would get here as soon as possible. However, we've been out of mobile range all our way here."

"It took us just over two hours," Narla said. "We didn't realise the track circled back around that deep cutting."

"You did well," Wyatt replied. "We were just stopping for a morning coffee. Come in. You must all be exhausted." He turned to his dog "Keep guard, Cinders," he ordered. "He's a great pet and perfect guard dog too. He saw you coming in before we did."

OVER COFFEE, THE NEWCOMERS told everything that happened at the hut.

"You did the right thing to call the police," Ellie said and nodded at her companion. "Annette here had her apartment blown up by Jaxon when he mistook her for me. Luckily, the bomb went off in the basement rather than on her floor and she survived. That's why the police are looking for him."

"Oh my God!" Scarlett gasped and gave Annette a gentle hug. "And how are you?"

Annette smiled. "Not too bad, thanks. There is still a bit to do on my arm but my face isn't too bad."

"I knew he was a bastard," Karson said.

"A bully and a coward," Narla added.

"That about sums him up," Ellie added. "He's stubborn, too."

"So we should leave," Wyatt said. "With that new storm coming, the creek will be up again." He glanced at Scarlett. "We can all fit in the Land Cruiser."

It really only took them a short time to load the Land Cruiser and lock the homestead up. It was a tight squeeze but Karson sat in the very back with Cinders, three sat on back seats and Ellie sat beside Wyatt at the front. Bags and packs filled up all the other space. As Wyatt drove out the drive, lightning flashed across the sky and thunder rumbled in the distance.

Moments later, they arrived at the stream but Ellie could see that they were too late. If anything, the torrent of water that flooded the road and the remains of the bridge was even higher than that first time they were there.

"It's pretty high," Wyatt said. "Swift, too. Do you want to cross?"

Ellie just stared out as the downpour arrived. "No," she said. "If we stalled half away over anything could happen."

"I agree," Karson almost shouted from the back so he could be heard above the noise of the storm. "Is there another way out?"

"No," Wyatt replied. "In summer at low tide, we could have driven along the beach but it's cliffs all the way to the next road out." He grimaced. "The tide is coming in, too so it'll get worse and with this storm..." He shrugged and never completed his sentence.

"So we go back to the homestead," Ellie said. "That's the safest place to go."

Wyatt turned to face those at the back. "Do you all agree?" he asked.

They did, so he reversed back to the same bend they'd used the first time. He turned the vehicle around and headed to the homestead.

Ellie sighed to herself. Of course, Jaxon may have left before the stream came up. She doubted if he had come all this way just on a motorbike so he would have had some sort of vehicle big enough to attach it onto. Knowing Jaxon, he'd be thinking of his own position before he though of anyone else.

"Yeah, you could be right," Wyatt said after she mentioned her thoughts to him. "With a little luck he'll run into the cops coming the other way."

"They could be close, too," Scarlett added. "Layla said they'd come out soon and that was early this morning."

WYATT DROVE SLOWLY using low ratio four-wheel drive as the torrential rain rocked the Land Cruiser from the ocean side to their left. The wipers and demister that were both on full speed could barely cope. Ellie peered out and attempted to help, as the road ahead was flooded in places.

"Keep going," she yelled when they came to a tight corner to the left. "You've got plenty of room on this side."

When Wyatt accelerated slightly out of the bend, stones pounded into the underside to compete with the noise of rain hitting the roof.

"Shut up, Cinders!" Wyatt yelled for the dog let out an excited howl as the Land Cruiser slid slightly. "We aren't just doing this for your fun."

Suddenly Ellie who had been momentarily distracted by Cinders stared out. There on the wrong side of the road was a camper van heading straight towards them. Luckily the driver had the vehicle's lights on or she wouldn't have seen it in the semi-darkness.

"Watch out!" she screamed.

Wyatt must have seen it at the same time for he pulled left as the other vehicle veered to the right and a horn blasted.

"Impatient bastard!" Wyatt retorted as he fought the bumping Land Cruiser with mud splattering up on Ellie's side.

It worked for the expected crash never eventuated. They must have missed the camper van by mere centimetres. The trusty Land Cruiser continued forward and the camper van disappeared around the bend behind them, still with its horn blasting.

Scarlet who was sitting on the right behind Wyatt reached forward and squeezed Ellie's arm. Ellie turned and saw wide eyes staring at her.

"It was Jaxon!" Scarlet gasped. "He had his head out the driver's window. I'd know him anywhere."

"That's true," Karson supported. "As he disappeared around the corner I saw the motorbike attached to the camper van's back bumper."

Ellie's mind twirled. There was no way that Jaxon and the camper van could get across the flooded stream. He would also be stuck on their side of the flooded stream!

WHEN WYATT DROVE THE Land Cruiser back around the back of the homestead he grimaced at Ellie after she had shut the main gate to the driveway behind them.

"My suggestion is that we make it appear that there is nobody here," he said. "We know your ex is capable of anything so trying to talk to him would be a waste of time."

"And how do we make it appear that way" Ellie replied.

"Firstly we park the Land Cruiser in the shed and keep away from the road. The hedges around pretty well hide the house from view." He shrugged. "I know that if he's determined it won't stop him."

He drove forward into a large outbuilding and explained that it was once the stables. Over recent years it became a garage and implement shed with space for several vehicles. In it was an truck-like quad bike, the lawn mower, the usual gardening gear plus a half assembled vintage truck.

"That's another of my projects," Wyatt said. "An old 1930s Ford V8. I had trouble getting parts and haven't done much on it for a couple of years."

It was still raining but not so heavily. This had the advantage that no tyre marks were left on the driveway. Also, once inside the house, the main living area was at the rear away from any street view. Scarlet, Narla and Karson accepted an invitation to stay and were allocated a couple of bedrooms upstairs, again picking those at the back. The front room blinds were left drawn, again to give an impression of the building being unoccupied.

The electricity was still operating so they settled into an almost normal situation of friends old and new staying there. Cinders enjoyed having so many humans to look after him and ran between everyone with his tail wagging. Anyone who was Wyatt's friend was also his friend, especially if they rubbed his ears or offered him food to eat.

"You'll spoil him," Wyatt laughed when Narla filled Cinder's food dish with dog food. "He never gets this attention when we're here by ourselves."

"Dogs can be such great company," she said.

LATER, THE RAIN STOPPED but it looked to be but a brief interlude as more black clouds hovered over the ocean. Ellie accompanied by Annette and Cinders took a chance to stretch their limbs by walking along the front boundary hedge. This hedge had been recently trimmed but was still higher than their heads. In places though the branches had been thinned so they could see the deserted road to their left. They had almost reached the boundary of Wyatt's property and intended to cross back at this point.

Cinders stopped and gave a low growl as he stared down the road in the direction of the beach.

"What is it Boy?" Ellie asked.

"Get back where we can't be seen." Annette gasped, grabbed Ellie's arm and tugged her back away from a gap in the hedge.

Ellie heard the sound before seeing a motorbike appear in the distance. As she watched she recognised Jaxon who wasn't wearing a helmet. It slowed as he went by and she gasped for he had his old hunting rifle slung across his back.

"Hush, Boy," Ellie said to Cinders and grabbed his collar. "Sit!"

The dog obeyed and looked up at her while Annette slunk back in a crouch. Ellie did the same for the motorbike stopped only a few metres from them. Had Jaxon seen them through the hedge?

Jaxon had one foot down to balance the bike as he peered around. For a second it seemed that he was directly looking at her before his eyes moved on. He glowered, muttered something to himself and moved the motorbike forward.

Ellie turned and noticed what Jaxon had probably seen. About fifteen metres away, the gate across the driveway that she had shut on the way in, was leaning forward slightly. In her haste in the rain she had neglected to pull a chain around. There in full sight was the unlocked padlock dangling from the chain.

Jaxon stopped right beside it, got off the motorbike, turned the engine off and walked to the gate. He moved it open slightly as he gazed towards the homestead.

"So you are here, you bitch!" he shouted.

Ellie trembled for she thought they had been seen. Annette's hand was shaking but she said nothing. Luckily, Cinders just sat as he'd been told but he was on full alert with is ears forward and he have one wag of his tail.

Meanwhile Jaxon just stood facing the homestead before he stepped back a little, possibly so he wouldn't be seen from anybody looking out. He actually reached back for his rifle but stooped, shrugged, returned to his motorbike and slowly rode it away back towards the beach from where he had come.

"He didn't want anyone to hear the bike," Annette said.

"It appears so," Ellie replied.

"If he came through the gate and turned our way he would have seen us. I was scared Cinders would bark!"

"He knew we wanted him to keep quiet," Ellie said and rubbed his ears. "Good Boy," she praised.

Cinders stood up, wagged his tail as if he understood the whole situation and gazed at her with intelligent eyes.

BACK IN THE HOMESTEAD, the six sat around the kitchen table discussing the news about Jaxon. Outside the expected follow-up storm had arrived with rain lashing the windows.

"Well he won't be doing anything now," Ellie said. "He isn't one who goes out in this weather."

Wyatt grimaced. "Which is the reason why he may be planning something right now. He knows you are familiar with his habits so could act out of character to fool you."

"I agree," Karson said. "The little contact I had with him showed a ruthless unpredictable character."

"We've done the basic things like locking the gate and house doors," Scarlett said. "What now?"

"I suggest that we leave," Wyatt suggested.

"And go where?" Ellie responded. "Didn't you say the stream loops back and the station houses are on the other side?"

"And Jaxon will be at the beach," Scarlett added.

"So we take the third choice," Wyatt added and explained his idea.

CHAPTER 12

Wyatt's suggestion was to leave and go to McArthur's Hut where they would be in mobile range of the outside world.

"It's too far. We'll never reach it before dark," Ellie responded.

"Not in the ATV," Wyatt said.

"What's that?" Scarlett asked.

"An All Terrain Vehicle, a Can-Am ATV that's more like a little truck than a motorbike. It has a partly closed in cab, a steering wheel rather than handlebars and a well-side tray at the back. Three can sit across the cab while the rest of you can ride in the tray. It'll be a tight squeeze but we'll fit."

"Cinders too?" Ellie asked.

"Of course," Wyatt replied.

Everyone agreed and after frantic packing and lock up the six were soon ready to go. Meanwhile Karson kept an eye on the road from behind the hedge. He returned to say there was no sign of Jaxon returning.

In spite of her protests, Annette was persuaded to squeezed in the front between Karson and Wyatt who was the driver while the other three sat in the tray. They were exposed but dressed for the weather that had dropped back to a drizzle. However further off, lightning and thunder told of more downpours to come.

Cinders jumped into the tray and snuggled in between the women's legs with his wagging tail hitting them all.

"Hang on," Wyatt called back. "Just bang the roof if you need me to stop for any reason. Sorry there's no seat belts for you."

"I doubt if there'll be any cops out here to ticket us," Ellie called back.

After driving across two paddocks with Karson opening and shutting the gates they reached the track that was also the boundary between the homestead and the rest of South Pacific View Station. Here, there was a double fence with the track wide enough for the ATV to fit between them.

"It is designed for maintenance vehicles like this one to use," Wyatt explained. "That is why there are no steps at this end." He glanced across sat Karson. "You know all about the track further up."

"Yeah, pretty narrow and steep in places. It's not as well maintained as the other tracks we used either."

"It's really just a branch track for those who want access to the beach and camping ground. Most of those who stay at the hut continue on to the next one. "

"That's what we were going to do," Karson replied.

They lapsed into silence after Wyatt reached the end of the farmlands and entered scrub country with a steep uphill section. Far below to the left, the cliffs were still in view with choppy waves pounding beneath them.

Ellie patted Cinders as they gripped a security rope attached to the tray top. Wyatt maintained a steady speed as he guided the vehicle along. With the engine and rain it was difficult to hear anything else but the pair's determination told in their expressions. She grinned at her two companions. Both were a decade younger than her and were far more confident than she ever was at their age.

The ATV reached an 'S' bend, wheels spun for a moment on a muddy section before Wyatt changed down a gear, corrected a minor slide and continued up the steep incline.

Having them all squeezed together actually helped as they held each other in a tight pack. Cinders in his wisdom, crawled back between everyone's legs and into a haven of warmth caused by their bodies. Ellie reached down and stroked his ears and felt his tail lash her legs.

"He's loving it, isn't he?" Narla called out

"Yeah, I wonder who are the dumb animals back here," Ellie replied.

"Hang on!" shouted Scarlett who was on the right side. "There's a tight bend coming up!"

It was a huge ninety-degree bend and for a moment all Ellie could see was the ocean and cliffs far below them. There appeared to be nothing but a massive drop. On the other side a sheer bank rose up to where massive trees grew.

She gulped! If they stalled now or slid sideways, there was nothing to stop them plunging down.

But they didn't!

The vehicle has built for this type of terrain and just putted on with smoke puffing out the exhaust and mud streaming up in an arch from the tyres.

They were now on a straight section beneath overhanging trees in the semi-darkness of overhead clouds between the foliage above. After several moments they came out of the trees with the ocean out of sight behind them. Ellie could now see the homestead way below her in the misty light.

The rain had stopped and a watery sun appeared for the first time. The ATV slowed and came to a halt on a small grassy bend.

"Thought you might like to stretch your legs. We're about half way there." Wyatt shouted back.

Ellie climbed down while Cinders took a chance to leap off the tray and disappear across the road to sniff around. Wyatt had a pair of binoculars that he looked through. Afterwards he held it held out for her.

"Thought we could have a look at the homestead. We'll drive out of sight soon and won't be able to see it again until we actually reach the hut," he said.

Ellie focused on the homestead and moved her field of vision across to the road. There near the hedge on the beach side she saw a parked motorbike. A man was almost invisible as he crouched down facing the homestead.

"It must be Jaxon," she said.

"That's what I thought," Wyatt replied. "I wonder if he saw us drive away."

"I doubt it, otherwise why would he remain hidden?" Ellie replied.

"Good point."

The others gathered around and all had a share of the binoculars to study Jaxon and the homestead.

"He's got something planned, that's for sure," Ellie said.

"Probably wait until it's dark before he makes a move," Karson added.

"Probably try the same tactics as with my apartment," Annette said. "Perhaps he'll set fire to the homestead or have another bomb."

"Unless he thinks the place is empty," Narla added.

"He knows we're on this side of the flooded stream," Ellie continued "With all this rain it must be still flooded." She turned to Wyatt. "Are we in mobile range yet?"

He shook his head. "We're still too far behind the main hill."

Scarlett produced a paper bag. "I found the apples and oranges in the kitchen and thought we might need something to munch," she said and handed the bag around.

Ellie grinned. Back at the homestead, she had been so busy gathering clothes and such like, she never thought about food for the journey. The trio as well as Annette were becoming real friends. Perhaps the crisis helped to bond them together.

"Right, we'll be off," Wyatt said

He whistled up Cinders who came running back and took an almighty jump onto the still empty tray, turned and glanced at everyone with his tail wagging. He was ready for his next adventure!

DUSK ARRIVED EARLY with the storm becoming violent as they continued their journey. Fork lightning flashed across the sky and thunder rumbled mere seconds later. Ellie knew that the lightning was roughly a kilometre away for every second that the thunder was heard so it was a safe distance away over the ocean to the southeast.

The rain arrived again plus a brief session of hail. The four on the tray, including Cinders huddled down and managed to ward off most of the stinging hail. Ellie's hands were frozen as she pulled her cape in closer around her neck. Her raincoat held out most water but drips still slid down beneath her collar and her jeans were soaked.

Her friends looked as saturated as she felt and it was only Cinders jammed in behind them who was barely affected.

"Stimulating isn't it?" Scarlet commented as water dripped off her eyebrows.

Ellie grinned. "Not quite the word I'd use but at least we aren't walking."

It was still raining heavily when they arrived at McArthur's Hut to find it empty. There was no sign of anyone having been there since they had left.

Ellie called the police on the mobile but Layla couldn't be contacted. She reported everything that had happened and was told more or less what they already knew. The police would be in the area as soon as possible, the weather hindered any helicopter flights and they were advised to stay where they were at McArthur's and make no attempt to contact Jaxon.

"So we're still on our own," she retorted.

"It's okay," Wyatt replied. "At least we can call out if necessary."

"I need to call, Mum," Scarlet said. "She worries so much, I'll just tell her we're back at the hut and she doesn't need to come out to pick us up."

After the initial rush with mobile calls to families and friends they settled into getting themselves organised. Their luggage that had been mainly in the cab beneath Annette and Karson's feet, was dry and with the fire now going they could relax and warm themselves. Wet coats strung across an internal line to dry and everyone assisted in setting up the bunks and starting a meal.

Outside the rain had stopped but a mist clung across the land below. Ellie realised how tired she and everyone else was. When hot water from the wetback in the fireplace was ready she waited while Annette had first shower followed by the other women and finally she had one herself.

IT WAS LATE AFTERNOON before Jaxon began his planned attack. He had everything sorted and a stiff whisky helped to calm his nerves as he checked his rifle and cartridges. The telescopic sight worked perfectly and he knew he had his ability from deer stalking days to be deadly accurate. Other details were worked out to precision and like a warrior going off into battle he started his motorbike and headed out.

Just out of the camping ground he turned inland rather than staying on the road. There he came to the track that headed towards McArthur's Hut with a roadside map showing details to the hut and beyond. He merely glanced at it to check whether his assumptions were correct. They were!

Soon the track became the double fence between the South Pacific View Station and the homestead. After a few minutes he was where he wished to be behind the homestead.

He grinned. They could watch the road as long as they liked but from here he could slip across a couple of paddocks without anyone in the homestead seeing him. Of course, he had to be sensible and study his surroundings. The misty rain actually helped for he doubt if anybody would be out the back.

He pushed his motorbike behind a small bank that hid it from anybody watching from the homestead direction, took his rifle and backpack of other gear and scanned the area with his binoculars. The area was empty and the top floor of the homestead that rose above the outer buildings also looked the same way. Curtains were pulled across the windows and there was no sign of movement. It was a slight risk, of course, but he doubted if anyone was inside was looking out.

There was that damn dog but the odds were that it would be with them or placed to watch the front gate. He found a shallow dip in the paddock further along to the right. This was a perfect place! From here he could see the back of the homestead and the driveway. Anybody running out in this direction would be a perfect target. He hoped there would be nobody but all possibilities had to be covered.

With adrenaline pumping through his body he took off his backpack,covered it with a small sheet of canvas he'd brought and pushed it into a dry area beneath some nearby shrubs. He slung the rifle across his back, grabbed his can of gas and headed in.

The implement shed was about a hundred metres across a lawn from the homestead and perfect for his plans. It was easy to break into from the back and provided the information he needed. There in the middle sat the Land Cruiser.

So they hadn't left! Great!

"Well Ellie, your days of being a bossy bitch will soon be over. And that new boyfriend will regret ever knowing you. There were the others too, he knew but they were collateral damage. Serve them right for thinking they could outwit him.

He laughed, slipped out of the shed and made his way across to the homestead. He unscrewed the top to the petrol can he had brought with him and poured the contents along a back wall. With tender dry wood over a century old it would be aflame within seconds.

Everything was still and silent inside but that was expected. The ignorant fools would not be expecting an attack from this direction. He took a small flask from a pocket and gulped down the last of the whisky. It was a cheap brand that tasted lousy but did the trick.

As darkness fell over the silent land it was all go!

AT MCARTHUR'S HUT, Ellie glanced up as the outside door flung open and Narla appeared after leaving a few seconds before to get an armful of wood.

"Get out here!" she cried in an almost hysterical scream and disappeared outside again.

Ellie jumped to her feet and along with everyone else tore out the door.

She saw it! Right where the homestead was in the valley below a ball of fire rose. Seconds later a faint rumble reached her ears.

"Bastard!" Wyatt swore from beside her. "I'll get you!"

Ellie flung her arm out to grab him but Wyatt brushed her aside and stalked towards the ATV. Ellie had never seen him act so determined with his jaw stuck out and both hands curled up in a punching position.

"No!" she screamed and ran behind him.

If he was determined, she was even more so for she guessed that he was about to take off in the ATV. If he did that there would be no way to stop him.

Instead of attempting to grab him, a movement that she knew would be futile for he was far too strong for her; she tore across the grass rather than sticking to the slightly curved path. In this way she out-paced Wyatt and reached the ATV seconds before he did

Her mind raced but she hoped that they would be there!

When she yanked the driver's door open she saw what she wanted.

The keys were in the keyhole. She pulled them out, stepped aside and ducked sideways just as Wyatt arrived.

He swung around, saw the keys in her hand and reached for them. But she was too fast. She dropped to her knees almost rolled sideways and avoided him.

"No," she cried. "It'll do no good! He's got a rifle and will kill you!"

Wyatt stopped still like a statue and just stared at her.

Ellie also stopped and faced him, still with the keys firmly clasped in her hand. She attempted to speak but emotions seized her. However, through shuddering tears that dripped off her quivering chin she managed to convey her feelings.

"You're all I've got, Wyatt," she sobbed. "I don't want to lose you. If Jaxon sees you coming and he will, he will not hesitate to shoot you."

Wyatt blinked back his own tears but the desperation in his eyes was gone. Instead they showed compassion and empathy as he stepped forward with his arms extended and seized her in a tight hug.

"You're right," he grunted. He reached down as she looked up and kissed her in a frantic kiss that she responded to.

The others arrived but just stood back in a semi-circle before Karson spoke.

"Ellie's right. What's a building compared with your life, Mate?" he asked

Ellie found she was trembling uncontrollably. She stepped back and found other arms around her. It was Annette who now held her while at the same time Karson placed an arm around Wyatt's shoulders.

"We'll call Layla and the police will catch him," Annette almost whispered.

"And we're safe," Scarlet added. "He does not know we're here."

"My God, I'm howling like a teenager," Ellie responded and placed the keys in her jeans pocket. There was no way she was going to give them up!

THIS TIME THEY DID reach Layla who listened to Ellie before Wyatt and Scarlett added to the coverage about what had happened. All they left out was the part about the keys. Finally, Ellie spoke to the detective sergeant again.

"You did the correct thing," Layla replied. "There is no way that you can reason with him. Don't leave McArthur's hut for any reason. We will come to you. Okay?"

"So what happens now?" Ellie replied

"Our Armed Defenders squad is on the way. They have an amphibious vehicle but were waiting until dawn. However, in the light of what has happened now, we'll advance the time and go across now. If Jaxon he attempts to go your way, we will stop him. The chances are is that he'll remain near the homestead but all scenarios will be covered.

I repeat, don't attempt to do anything, even if you see him. Take the usual precautions of remaining out of sight. We have a helicopter available when the weather improves. Zack or myself will keep in touch. One other point, please don't call any news outlets. The last thing we need is for Jaxon to hear a news item and find out you're all alive and okay."

"We've only contacted friends and family," Ellie replied. "I hope that was okay. Everyone here is very discrete."

"Thank you. I'm glad you are so sensible in such a dangerous situation," Layla replied before she finished the call.

"So did Narla get that wood for the fire?" Karson asked to break the silence that followed. "I reckon it'll get cold tonight."

CHAPTER 13

Jennifer Sigley was beginning to regret her decision to visit the homestead after she had found that Wyatt would be there over the weekend. She really wanted evidence to support her claim to half the estate and had actually rented a beach cottage at Greystone Beach for the weekend. Her idea was to confront him and that hussy that he had shacked up with. No doubt the woman was just a money grabber preparing to bleed Wyatt dry. Rumours were that she was a schoolteacher and everyone knew how little they got paid.

But now the weather had turned terrible but even worse was the road. She had always visited the area in summer and had forgotten how bad it was. She had no idea what she'd do if she met a vehicle coming the other way. However so far, the road remained empty. She guessed that even the local farmers would be too sensible to be out in this weather.

Her Mercedes though now five years old, could handle the rod well though. When her claim for half the homestead was won she'd be able to buy a new one.

Jennifer grinned as she remembered the salesman telling her that the Mercedes could handle any outback New Zealand road. She drove slowly around a corner to find a flooded stream ahead with what looked like the remains of the bridge sticking up through the raging water. She stopped before a large sign that stated the obvious that the bridge was closed. An arrow directed her to where the stream could be forded. She pulled her raincoat close and walked over to the water's edge. There was the beginning of a concrete section but the rest was dirty brown water swirling through.

Oh damn it; she had a good car so she'd try it. If the worse came to worse she could back out and there was enough room on this side to turn around. She climbed back in, selected the Low rather than Drive mode and headed in. The rev. dial spun up as she hit the water.

The water outside shot up like an inverted waterfall so she did the logical choice. She turned the wipes to full speed and accelerated forward.

My God, what was she doing? All she could see was water everywhere. The car sort of swayed and she could barely see the far side. Luckily the car was a heavy one and the salesman did say it could go anywhere. She vaguely remembered that if the exhaust pipe got covered in water the car would stall but it was too late now. Instead, she pushed the accelerator to the floor in grim determination and kept going.

When the engine spluttered, her confidence evaporated but she held on. There was a shudder but the far side was close. Wheels gripped and she could see the concrete above the waterline.

She had reached the far side! She had done it!

Once back on the original gravel road she slowed and stopped, wiped her shaking hands on her jacket and grinned. She doubted if even Wyatt could have done it any better.

Also, even the rain had stopped. She climbed out, took off her saturated raincoat and reached for a dry jersey from the back seat. There was also a thermos of hot coffee there that she unscrewed and gulped down. She loved coffee and seldom drank anything stronger.

The car looked fine so she climbed back in and continued her journey towards the beach.

JENNIFER DECIDED TO visit the homestead before going to the beach. It looked no different and was reasonably tidy with a mown lawn and trimmed hedge. No doubt Wyatt paid a local to keep it tidy. The gardens, though were just weeds with not even the roses she remembered planting a few years back surviving. Mind you, at today's prices it would be worth a million bucks if some overseas entrepreneur bought it as a summer retreat.

The place appeared empty so she headed to the Greystone Beach Village. God it looked awful, more like a ghost town than a living community. There was nobody there; the local shop that was a hive of activity in summer with teenagers sitting around guzzling beer and so forth was closed. She stopped and read a faded sign that read *Closed for the winter season. See you in December.*

The camping ground was empty but did look cared for. A camper van was parked by a cottage but again nobody was around, She guessed that trampers had headed into the hills. She shuddered for she hated being alone. She reached for her mobile and glanced at the screen. Damn she had forgotten that the place was out of range. She could however access messages she had downloaded earlier.

She did so and found the formation needed. The cottage she had rented was Number 17 on Beach Road. The only other parallel road was called Seaview Road. The camping ground was actually beyond 17 so she drove back the few hundred metres and found it.

The cottage was at the back of a large front lawn that had been recently mowed and had a well-tended flower garden with flowers and little shrubs. There was no garage but plenty of parking space on the lawn. The note on her message told her where the key was, how to turn the electricity on and other basic details.

After going inside, she pulled back the curtains but left the sliding patio door shut because of the rain. At least it was now just drizzling, not that horrible earlier thunderstorm. Everything worked in the batch and she relaxed a little as she unpacked and made herself a meal.

She decided not to bother to confront Wyatt and the woman until the morning. Also it appeared that they hadn't arrived anyway and perhaps they had even decided not to come because of the weather. She grimaced but she was here now. If they weren't there, in the morning she could look around the homestead for she still had her keys to the place.

It was getting late and would soon be dark. When she walked out to get a few more things from the car she heard an engine roaring and glanced up as a guy on motorbike roared by. Where did he come from?

She grimaced. Probably it was a local worker from the station. She knew the road went a couple of kilometres further along the coast before stopping at the South Pacific View Station wool shed. She shrugged, walked back inside and turned on the television. At least she could get the main channels on it.

JENNIFER JERKED UP and realised that she must have fallen asleep on the couch. It was almost dark outside but something else was different. She could smell smoke and there was a red glow out a side window.

She rushed out the back door and stared. My God, the sky was lit up by a red glow inland. Something was on fire and wasn't that the direction of the homestead!

She found her shoes, grabbed her coat and tore out to the car.

Moments later she arrived to see that the back of the homestead was on fire. It was not just a tiny blaze but the whole rear section was a towering inferno of flames twice as high as the building itself. She swung into the driveway but screeched to a stop when she realised that to go any closer would be too dangerous.

"No," she screamed. "Not the homestead!'

The noise of crackling wood, the heat and the smell of smoke engulfed her when she stepped out. Shaking and not knowing what to do she just stood there trembling. Nobody appeared from the homestead but surely they could see the fire! Agonising thoughts filled her mind. Where was Wyatt? Was he or anyone else inside?

Perhaps they hadn't arrived yet.

She decided that she had to look. However, it was hopeless going too close because of the intense heat and also flying debris and the smoke. She circled across the front lawn with the aim of getting to the front door. Suddenly, out of the blackness she saw the silhouette of a man rise before you. Her eyes focused on him and she screamed. He had a rifle that was aimed straight at her.

"Just stop, you stupid bitch!" the man snarled. 'Take one more step and it'll be the last you ever make."

She stopped, terrified. "Who are you?" she managed to scream.

'Your worst nightmare lady," he replied. "Cooperate and you might just survive the night. Who I am is of no concern to you for I'm more interested in knowing who the hell you are and what you're doing here.

Jennifer gulped down air and found herself unable to breathe. She staggered and fell to her knees as the world around spun. The sensation of her throbbing grazed knees and water-soaked skirt made rational thoughts bring her back from a semi-delirious state.

"Get up!' the man commanded. "If I was going to shoot you I would have done it by now. Calm down and answer my question."

"Question! What question?" Jennifer howled. "This is my homestead that is on fire."

"Yours?" The man sounded angry again. "Who are you?"

"Jennifer Sigley. I own this property."

'I know the surname so how do you connect to Wyatt Sigley, that real estate guy?" His voice now sounded almost calm.

"He's my husband!" Jennifer stuttered. "Well he was. We're divorced now."

"Oh I see," the man retorted. "Now isn't this an interesting situation." He raised the barrel of his rifle ever so slightly. "We, perhaps have something in common."

"What's that?" Jennifer asked. For a moment curiosity overcame her fear.

"It seems that your husband has shacked up with my wife. Now you can help me for I was waiting for them. Do you know where they are?"

Jennifer screamed at the man. "You lit the fire, didn't you?"

"No you stupid bitch, you did!" He grinned. "Perfect, isn't it? Jealous wife wants revenge and sets fire to the family homestead.""

"But it'll be a lie!" Jennifer retorted, terrified again

The man's voice was like ice. "Just do exactly what I say, Mrs Jennifer Sigley." He glanced up. "You must be staying somewhere there. Is that true?'

"I've hired a summer cottage for the weekend."

"Good. There's nothing more we can do here so we'll go home to your place and discuss your future." He smiled sarcastically. "Why your ex would give up an attractive gal like you for my mousy wife amazes me."

Jennifer froze. This guy wasn't only an arsonist but a psychopath. She'd have to be extremely careful not to antagonise him. She thought she was in danger of being shot but the situation was now worse far worse than even that.

And there was nobody around who could help. She was entirely alone!

THE OPPORTUNITY CAME when the guy forced her to get in the Mercedes.

"I have to back out," Jennifer said to him as he stood outside the car with his rifle aimed at her. "It is too dangerous to go any closer to the fire."

He glanced back at the long driveway and the muddy looking lawns. Jennifer could almost read his thoughts. If the car turned onto them the chances were that it would get stuck.

"Okay, " he said in that returned calm voice. "Just don't do anything silly while I walk around to the passenger seat."

"I'm not stupid," Jennifer muttered but discreetly moved the automatic gear lever.

With his rifle still aimed at her he walked around the front of the car probably so that he could keep her in view.

Without hesitation, Jennifer pushed the accelerator down and the car responded by moving forward as she expected. The guy was sideswiped with an almighty bump and he was flung back out of sight; there was a sound of the rifle being fired but nothing more.

She braked, found "R' and swung the steering wheel out to avoid the still out-of-sight man. With her eyes glued on the reversing screen she could see him sprawled to the ground but bringing the rifle around. He disappeared from view as the slight curve of the driveway zoomed ahead before her. She was going too fast!

The car wobbled as the right side hit grass, she corrected and lurched to the left, an outside wheel spun for a second but returned to the concrete. There was another bump and Jennifer slid down behind the steering wheel... the windscreen shattered as another bullet ricocheted through the car but only glass fragments hit her.

Sheer adrenalin kept her going as bile built in her throat and her heart raced. She wobbled the steering wheel and the car responded. There was another report but nothing hit the Mercedes, the hedge and gateposts lit up under the glare of the reversing lights followed by a screeching sound.

Oh hell, she had sideswiped the far post. Again she corrected the steering, reached the road, swung the car to the right and braked. She found "L' instead of 'D' but this actually helped for the engine screamed as the car roared forward with the rev meter hitting the red zone.

She realised she was facing away from the beach and heading for the flooded stream but she didn't care. Freezing air hit her face from the broken windscreen hole and she found she couldn't see forward. There was only the clouded glass with the jagged spot where the bullet had come through. She was too terrified to stop but did have the sense to slow as she peered through the hole. Damn, she had not turned on the headlights!

With a shaking hand she switched them on and sighed in relief as the road ahead lit up. It was almost like a friend and a complete contrast to the rear vision mirror view that showed the burning homestead behind her.

"I did it Wyatt," she gasped. "Aren't you proud of me?"

Damn it! Why did she always think back to him when there was trouble?

SHE WAS ALMOST BACK at the flooded stream when she glanced in her rear vision mirror.

There was one single light from behind rapidly gaining on her. Oh damn, it must be that guy on a motorbike. Who else could it be?

She reached forward to the hole in the windscreen and ignoring sharp edges, yanked out a large section that ended up on her lap. A cold wind now tore in but at least she could see. She accelerated and had the satisfaction of seeing the light behind fall further back.

Once she reached the stream she'd drive right in. If the car did it before it would do it again. Anyway what else could she do?

The headlight behind was now coming closer!

Seconds later and with a mighty crack the back window shattered, she heard a whine of something near her ear and the distant report of a rifle shot.

Terrified she accelerated but something hit her upper right arm. Pain arrived and her sleeve became soaked in something sticky. She felt dizzy when she realised that she must have been shot.

She had to get to the stream; it must be close!

Her right side became numb and her arm just sort of flopped around. When she attempted to move it excruciating pain shot though her whole side. She used her left hand to grip the wheel and managed to steer the car around a bend.

There before her was the stream but it was lit up by circle of floodlights set up on the far bank. Even better was the flashing blue lights on a vehicle on her side of the stream. It was a white and blue truck on four massive tyres and the words *Police Rescue* emblazoned along one side.

"Oh My God! Oh My God!" she gasped.

She braked but failed to hold the steering wheel with her one good hand. Her car careered across the road, hit a bank and tipped.

All Jennifer could remember was a screeching sound and pain as her seatbelt held her and an airbag inflated around her. She was on her side; the whole car as on its side and crumbled metal crushed her body.

She'd beat the bastard though. He'd meet his match if he tried to shoot at the cops.

She managed to grin to herself just before she lost consciousness.

JAXON CURSED WHEN THE car failed to stop. He was sure he'd hit the bitch but she seemed to be able to take the bend. The stream must be close and there was nowhere for her to go!

The car taillights disappeared but beyond the trees the sky was lit up and it was obviously more than the car headlights. He slowed slightly and followed her behind the bend.

He swore for floodlights lit up the entire area! Before him with blue lights flashing was a gigantic vehicle. He managed to stop and just watch as the Mercedes cut across the road, hit the side of the cliff, toppled, skidded back in a shower of sparks and came to a stop on its side.

He waited for the car to explode but it didn't! Could the bitch still be alive?

He saw people in riot gear running towards the car. Someone looked up and pointed at him sitting there. He'd better get away and now!

Ignoring a bullhorn blearing out for him to stop, he turned and accelerated away, suddenly concerned about his own safety and the woman momentarily forgotten. His well thought out plans had vanished. Somebody would have to pay for this!

Nobody got the better of Jaxon Parkes, nobody! It was a setback but he'd survive. There was just one more bitch to add to his list.

CHAPTER 14

Late that night in the tiny bathroom away from the others, Ellie and Wyatt made love. For the first time in years she felt fulfilled and the act wasn't something she had to tolerate. Wyatt was so gentle at first until all the frustrations of their situation just evaporated. She rose to the occasion as they came together in a frenzied demonstration of their affection.

"Oh my God," Ellie gasped afterwards. "I hope we didn't awaken the others with all our moaning."

Wyatt grinned, "Who cares. I know Scarlet and Karson were in here earlier."

"Shameful," Ellie said in mock disgust. "The modern generation, you know."

"I know." Wyatt stepped forward, grabbed her arm and pulled her into the shower cubical. There under the steaming water they made love again, something Ellie had never done in her life before.

This time little was said as they dried each other down and went back into the living area, She found her jersey to slip on for it was really quite cold in the room. Wyatt took her hand and they walked out to the path. It was pitch dark but the rain had stopped. Way in the valley below there was no homestead but just a circle of embers and smoking ashes.

"The homestead's gone," she gasped. "It looks as if your Land Cruiser and everything else in the shed have gone, too."

Wyatt stared at her with trembling lips. "At least nobody was inside," he whispered.

Ellie glanced at her watch that was still on her wrist. It was just after three in the morning.

DAWN ARRIVED WHEN ELLIE and Wyatt walked into the living area to find the fire roaring and Annette and Narla sitting at the table having breakfast.

"You two are as bad as the others," commented Annette as she scooped up some cornflakes. "Interruptions during the night, I guess."

Ellie felt her cheeks burn in embarrassment. "Went to see if the fire was still burning," she muttered

"For sure," Narla chuckled. "Don't worry, I'm used to discretely leaving Scarlet and Karson and getting breakfast."

Wyatt's mobile rang and he answered.

"Hello Layla," he said and switched on the speaker on so they could all hear.

"There have been developments. Did you know Jennifer was in the district?"

"No. What was she doing here?"

"I thought you might be able to tell us that," the detective sergeant replied. "She's in hospital recovering from a gunshot wound."

"What?" Wyatt gasped.

Ellie and everyone else listened as Layla told them everything she knew.

"We haven't managed to find Jaxon even though we have officers searching for him. My real reason for this call is to warn you that he might try to reach you. With his motorbike, he could be there at any time."

"But he doesn't know we're here," Ellie cut in.

"Our theory is that he thought you were in the homestead and planned to shoot anyone who ran out from the fire," Layla continued. "If anyone had been inside there was no hope that they would have escaped. The place was tender dry and only took seconds to be engulfed in flames."

"Thanks," Wyatt replied. "So you're pretty sure Jaxon started the fire?"

"Yes. He used an accerant, probably petrol rather than an explosive device. That was all that was needed for such an old wooden structure."

"If he arrives what can we do?" Ellie gasped.

"My advice is to retreat back to hide in the bush. We have arranged for the Life Flight Rescue Helicopter to come as soon as possible to evacuate you all. The storm is over but a morning fog is still hindering helicopter flights throughout the region. We'll keep in touch."

She rung off and Ellie glanced around to see everyone deep in thought,

"We could keep going in the ATV," Karson said. "It's pretty steep but we should be able to drive at least half the distance back to Woolstone Hut."

"They've been widening it from this end over the last few years," Wyatt explained. "There is also that side branch to Riversdale Beach."

"But if Jason arrives after we left he'd know someone has been here," Narla said. "If he followed us his motor bike he could catch us up."

"Unless we block the track," Annette suggested.

"How?" Ellie asked.

Annette shrugged. "I don't know. Cut a tree down over it or something."

Wyatt grinned. "Great thinking Annette," he said. "My chainsaw is in the ATV's tool box."

THE TREES THAT WERE close to the track were too large to fell. However, Wyatt solved the problem by cutting off an overhanging branch that landed by the track. Between them all it wasn't too difficult to drag it across the track.

"Jaxon will have trouble shifting it by himself," Ellie commented as she examined the leafy branches that completely blocked the way.

They walked back to the hut and after a brief discussion decided to take the ATV a few hundred metres up the track to where there was a grassy section before a steep climb through dense bush.

Once there, Wyatt drove the ATV behind trees. It wasn't really hidden from anything but a casual view but there was nowhere else. They walked into the trees, climbed a steep bank that opened out to a point of knee high grass. The homestead site was out of sight but there was one brief part of the lower track visible. The rest of the view showed the ocean waves rolling in towards the shore. In different circumstances it would be wonderful scene.

The mobiles were still in range and another call to Layla really just confirmed what they knew. Thick fog in Wellington still grounded the helicopter but with the search for Jaxon in full swing they were not in immediate danger,

Layla sounded grumpy after being told about the felled branch. "Stay away from it," she almost ordered.

"We are," retorted Wyatt. He raised his eyebrows at Ellie and after the call was over muttered. "Damn cops think everyone is an idiot."

JAXON ASSUMED, QUITE correctly as it turned out, that there would be nobody at the station woolshed at the end of the road. This was not the main woolshed and was rarely used at this time of the year. Way back it was the only one on the property and a long-gone wharf had facilities for a barge that carried wool bales out to an awaiting coastal boat.

He drove the camper van with his motorbike on the back around behind the building and into an attached shed. A quick search around found the main power switch. Good, the electricity was still connected. He plugged in the camper van but resisted turning on any lights. He did though have the heater and stove working so could have a comfortable night. The radio news never mentioned anything about the homestead fire. Probably it was of low priority on all the radio networks that he had access to.

Morning arrived with the storm mainly over. The ocean was still quite rough with waves pounding the shore with an approaching high tide. Jaxon ignored the view and considered what he should do. Nothing was turning out as it should, the whisky had gone and he was down to his last can of beer. Well he might as well drink it for breakfast.

He knew it would be hopeless trying to drive out along the road. Cops and fire fighters would be everywhere so the only other alternative was the track up to McArthur's Hut. He had been beyond it in his deer stalking days and remembered that the track had another deviation that wound back several kilometres to Riversdale Beach, the largest settlement on this coast. From there he could go wherever he wished.

He drove out and along to a nearby parking bay and left the camper van at the beginning of the track. This was much more logical that attempting to hide it somewhere. It was not unusual for vehicles used by trampers and hunters to be left there. With tank topped up with fuel from a can he'd brought with him and other supplies in a backpack, he headed out to McArthur's Hut on the motorbike.

It was still early and the most dangerous spot would be along behind the homestead. It seemed quiet there, though and he'd done a reasonable job for nothing was left of the building or implement shed, just ashes and bits of debris remained. There was still a fire engine, a cop car and another vehicle there. As well a small tent that had been erected near the driveway. He saw nobody and assumed that anybody looking out would think he was just a farm worker going by.

Fifteen minutes later, Jaxon's planning was cut off when he came to a corner to see a gigantic branch had fallen right across the track. Swearing about how this could possibly happen he found the branches of leaves were higher than his head and the main branch was too heavy to shift.

Fuming, he walked along and made two discoveries; he could see where the whole branch had been dragged across the gravel and even worse was that the end had not just snapped off in the storm. It had been sawn though. Somebody had purposely done this!

"Bastards!" he muttered. It would be Ellie's boyfriend. No woman could move such a large branch. So the bitch and the guy she had shacked up with weren't in the homestead after all!

He attempted to pivot the branch around to make enough room for the motorbike to get by but the upper bushy side as held in place by trees and the base section would hardly move.

There was no way to get the motorbike past!

What could he do?

He realised he could continue on by foot but McArthur's Hut would be about an hour's walk away. Alternatively, he could go back to where the cops were waiting. He sat down on a clump of grass and thought of another possibility. If he went back out of the bush there were the top paddocks of the South Pacific View Station that led down to the beach. He could cut across them and reach the beach. It would be just after high tide now and the cliffs at both ends of Greystone Beach were impassable.

However, when the tide became lower he could ride the motorbike most, if not all the way below the cliffs to Riversdale Beach, his original destination. Ebb tide would be mid-afternoon so he'd have plenty of time.

After cursing Ellie and all women in general, he headed back out of the forest and soon reached the top paddocks. Yes, he could see the beach and the faint line of wet sand to show where the high tide waves had retreated. He'd make his way to the beach and wait awhile for the tide to retreat further. The waves were still pounding the shore but shouldn't affect him.

At least something was working in his favour.

THE TRACK BEYOND MCARTHUR'S Hut where Ellie and the others set off to follow was steep and slippery. In one section, everyone had to climb out of the ATV except for Wyatt who was driving. Karson pulled a winch wire from the front bumper and attached it to a tree trunk higher up the track. When Wyatt wound it slowly up everyone helped to guide the vehicle as spinning wheels shot mud everywhere. Even Cinders joined in and with his tail wagging, barked if the inside wheels got too close to an inside ditch.

"Oh my God, you all look like mud babies," Annette laughed from her position near the top to guide them.

"Yeah," Ellie responded as she lifted a muddy strand hair from across her face. "If you think we look bad you should see Cinders."

The dog barked in delight and jumped though a mud pile so deep he was almost swimming by the time he reached Annette.

Finally, the ATV reached a ridge at the top, everyone clamoured aboard and they continued on. Ten minutes later they reached a fork with a sign pointing to Riversdale Beach to the right and Woolstone Hut, left.

Wyatt walked with Ellie along the Riversdale Fork and rubbed his chin. "I reckon we can get through," he said. "This side actually looks wider than the other way. It's mainly downhill, too."

Back at the ATV, they had a coffee from the thermos and continued on after contacting Layla to say where they were. The new track wound back towards the coast and at one point followed it across a comparatively flat area above the cliffs. Below them was the ocean with pounding waves almost reaching the shore. The rain had stopped but low cloud covered the sky.

"STOP!" ELLIE CRIED from her position at the back of the ATV and thumped on the cab roof.

"What is it?" Wyatt shouted back as the vehicle came to a halt.

"There's someone down there in that little bay between those two points." Ellie pointed to a section where the beach was visible below the cliffs.

Wyatt climbed out of his seat and came around to stand beside her. He squinted and had to shade his eyes from the early morning sun that shone through a break in the clouds.

He reached for his binoculars that were dangling around his neck and peered through them.

"Guess who it is?" He handed the binoculars to her.

It took her a few seconds to find a guy standing beside a motorbike but when she did she grimaced. It appeared that he was stuck for the headland ahead was all rocks with no room for the motorbike at all.

"It's definitely Jaxon and it looks like he's stuck there," she said and reached for her mobile. "I'll call Layla."

She muttered an oath when she found her mobile was out of range again.

"Well, he's going nowhere except back on his motorbike," Scarlet now had the binoculars and confirmed who it was.

"If he turns back he could find a road in," Wyatt added. "I think the closest would be at Flat Point but there may be others."

"So we'll reach Riversdale before him?" Ellie asked.

Wyatt nodded. "The roads in are like our one and don't go to Riversdale," he said. "Once inland there are other local roads he could take and escape any police road blocks."

"It sounds like his luck," Ellie muttered. "At least we know where he is."

FAR BELOW THE CLIFFS, Jaxon was unsure about what to do. After travelling for almost half an hour he came to this new point that was a mass of jagged rock with the waves crashing over the outer section He could climb his way past but there was no way to get the motorbike through. When the high tide returned the area he was now in would be under water. Also, without a map he had no idea how far away Riversdale Beach was or where any roads went.

Movement above the cliff caught his eye and saw one of those farm vehicles stop. Several people gathered in a line and it was obvious that they could see him. They were too far away for him to recognise but wasn't it logical that it was Ellie and those others he'd met at the hut. There was even that damn dog running around with them. Perhaps if he used the telescopic sights on his rifle he might see her. He aimed it but even when viewing with the telescopic sight he was still unsure whether anyone up there was Ellie for the women, he guessed they were, all had their faces shielded by the rain clothes they wore.

They were within range of his rifle but the chance of hitting anyone was remote. He watched as they all climbed back aboard their vehicle that drove away. Jaxon thought back and remembered a road that followed the beach a few kilometres back. It had appeared to be going in the wrong direction. Also, at that time he was making good progress, the tide was still going out so he'd ignored it.

Now the situation was different. If he went back to that road it could be the one that the vehicle was on. If it wasn't he could travel inland and find his way out of this God forsaken place. He grinned, started his motorbike and headed back south.

Again, everything was working out okay. With a little luck he'd get his bitchy ex and the woman who had attempted to run him down. Both bitches deserved to be punished and he'd get them later if not sooner.

DETECTIVE SERGEANT Layla Fraser and a dozen or more police officers and fire fighters had reached the homestead where boths buildings had been razed. In the implement shed all that remained were the burnt out hulks of two vehicles and other non-combustible items. The fire fighters were now hosing down the smoking embers for there is little else they could do.

Noel, one of the civilians from the police van came up to her. He was a likeable young guy who was in charge of technical surveillance and had brought in one of the latest drones the police were using.

"We've got them all, Layla." Unlike most of the police officers he ignored her rank, not that she minded. "Close but safely apart. Have a look at our drone's view. This is live." He handed her an iPad.

She glanced at a zoomed in video of Jaxon on the beach next to a motorbike. The view zoomed out to show an ATV on the cliff top with six people and dog gathered around looking down at Jaxon below. She recognised Ellie and Wyatt but not the others in another zoomed in view.

"So how come they're so close?"

Noel took back the iPad and switched to a Google map that named roads, tracks and farm buildings. He highlighted a track that included McArthur's hut and the area around. "They're on this sidetrack that leads to Riversdale Beach," he said. "Jaxon is attempting to get there, too by using the beach while the tide is out." He grimaced. "He obviously has no knowledge of the coastline for even if he can get his motorbike through or continue on foot there are several more headlands ahead with one that is impassable even at low tide."

He returned to the live view that showed two developments. Jaxon was on his motorbike travelling back while Ellie and the others had returned to their ATV and continued on towards Riversdale Beach.

"They'll have the same problem," Noel said.

"And that is?"

"The track returns to a steep forested section before circling back and down to Riversdale. It is narrow and includes steps. There is no way their ATV will be able to get through." Noel frowned. "The problem is that if Jaxon goes back to Flat Point Road, the track off from it leads to where the ATV is. The tracks are well signposted so he'll realise he can get onto their track.

"So he'll be able to catch up to them before we can?"

"Exactly. "

Layla frowned. She spoke on her satellite phone that had coverage in this remote area and nodded grimly. The situation was becoming serious.

CHAPTER 15

Ellie wondered why Wyatt had stopped until she glanced around the side of the ATV and saw the reason. The track that had scarcely been wide enough for the vehicle was now surrounded by trees and ferns. She grimaced at the others and slid off the tray, walked ahead by brushing away ferns and almost collided with Wyatt who had climbed out of the driver's seat.

He grinned and tucked an arm around her shoulders, "At least that's something," he said.

Ellie followed his gaze and saw a set of steps winding up through the foliage. There was also a wooden side rail. The others gathered around silently but their expressions told it all. They varied from grim annoyance to Karson who just shrugged. The only joyful one was Cinders who gave a woof and disappeared up the steps. He reappeared a moment later and wagged his tail as if to say that everything was fine.

Narla broke the impasse by rubbing Cinders' ears and giving a little laugh. "Look on the bright side, Guys," she said. "It's stopped raining and we must be less than an hour's walk from Riversdale."

"So what about the ATV?" Ellie asked.

"It won't be going anywhere," Wyatt replied. "After all the fuss is over I can come back for it." He waved back along the track. "If I reverse to that corner, I'll be able to turn it around ready to head back."

After a long rigorous climb up the steps they came to a narrow track that hugged a cliff on one side with a steep drop on the other. Across a ravine was more forest with the only other view being that of the sky with wisps of blue showing through a thin cloud layer.

Ellie, who had slipped back to the rear of their line to get an annoying stone out of a sandal, had Cinders for company. He sat below her as she took a sandal off and removed the stone.

Cinders glanced back behind them, stopped wagging his tail, his ears lowered and he growled.

"What is it, Boy?" Ellie asked.

She studied the steep track they had just come up that consisted of a long curved section with a sharp corner further back. It appeared deserted but was it? She squinted and saw movement. Someone appeared to slink around the corner. He stepped out, stopped and retreated out of sight. Even with that fleeting glance she knew who it was.

"Wyatt," she hissed to her partner a few metres ahead. "Jaxon's following us!"

This was instantly confirmed when a rifle shot echoed through the trees. Cinders leaped up and she grabbed his collar to stop him charging off. "No, Boy. Stay! He's got a gun."

Wyatt stepped back, grabbed her hand and with Cinders beside them, they ran forward to where the others waited.

"Just go!" Wyatt called. "That was Jaxon who shot at us."

There was no panic but grim determination as they ran forward, and helped each other up steep or slippery parts. Annette was having trouble and slipped, Karson stepped back and helped her to her feet. He guided her forward as Ellie joined them.

"Sorry," Annette sobbed. "When I slipped I bumped my sore arm. Just go on. I'll be okay."

"No," Ellie replied. "We stay together. Guard Annette, Cinders."

The dog knew what to do. He stepped in beside her, looked up, thumped his tail once and kept with her as Karson held her good hand to assist.

Scarlett came back. "Narla's come to the top. There are trees everywhere but on the right it slopes upwards. She thinks we could get behind trees on the left and hide."

Seconds later they all joined Narla but Wyatt frowned. "It's too obvious," he said.

Ellie could see his reasoning. Ahead the track was straight with no way to reach the other end before Jaxon appeared. However, if he saw it was empty he would know they had gone into the trees.

"We should go up the steep side," she suggested.

There was no hesitation. They turned and headed upwards, using low tree branches to pull themselves up. Karson practically lifted Annette in one part while Ellie steadied her by clutching her good arm. Annette squinted back tears of pain but was determined and kept going. They moved up in a diagonal direction for about thirty metres before Narla, who was still in the lead stopped beside a row of flax that towered above their heads.

"In here?" she gasped.

"Yes!" Ellie whispered back.

It was like a tunnel beneath the flax but with room for them all as long as they stayed in single file. Cinders remained just behind Annette the whole time. He was told to guard her and nothing would stop him carrying out his orders.

The flax must have been originally planted in a line for they came out the other side into an outcrop of tall grass. Everyone stopped, lay down and again without any instructions wiggled forward so they would not show their heads above the grass. Ellie arrived and found that by parting the grass she could see the track below them.

Jaxon appeared looking frustrated and exhausted. She knew he was not fit and the climb and his temperament showed in his behaviour. He stopped, slung his rifle off his shoulders and stared around.

"Bastards!" he howled. "You think you can get away by hiding in the trees."

Ellie jumped in fright as he raised his rifle and fired three rapid shots. The noise of the discharges seemed to be magnified by the surroundings and was so loud that her ears rung.

Shivering, she noticed that he had his back to them and was firing in the opposite direction. She had anticipated his thoughts correctly. If they had gone the other way, one of them could have been shot.

Jaxon fired three more shots but again they were all fired in the opposite direction.

"Ellie you cowardly bitch," Jaxon shouted. "'Come on out and I'll leave the others alone. I know you're all there. I can wait." He lowered his rifle. "If you agree to come back home we could start again."

"Like hell and high water," Ellie whispered and felt Wyatt's hand squeezing her one.

"Look up," he whispered in her ear.

She did so and gasped. Over the track between the trees and above Jaxon hovered a drone. The police had been following him the whole time!

A voice boomed out from a loudhailer. "Jaxon Parkes, this is Detective Sergeant Layla Fraser of the New Zealand Police. You are to place your rifle down and place your hands on your head or suffer any consequences. No other warning will be given."

Jaxon looked up. "Bastards!" he yelled and fired at the drone.

Ellie heard two reports but one sounded different. It was more of a high-pitched whine. She noticed an orange flash come from the drone. Jaxon staggered, screamed and crashed to the ground. The police had shot him remotely from the drone.

"'Deadly!" Wyatt remarked.

Silence followed. Jaxon sort of quivered for a moment before he remained still on the track below.

CONFLICTING EMOTIONS engulfed Ellie as, ignoring the others, she raced down and across to Jaxon. The right side of his shirt was saturated with blood. Trembling, she reached forward and felt for a pulse. Yes, he was still alive but for how long, she had no idea. Gulping, she looked closer and saw the wound. Blood was gushing out from beneath his right shoulder.

She linked the fingers of her hands and pushed down on the wound in an attempt to stop the flow. It worked, too.

"He's still alive," she said when she realised Wyatt was beside her.

"I think they were aiming at his right arm so he couldn't use his rifle," Wyatt said.

'Is he alive?" called Layla's distinctive voice over the loudhailer. "Hold your arms high if he is and wide if he is dead."

"I'll do it." Scarlett stepped back, faced the drone and held her arms high.

'The rescue helicopter is on its way and will be there in fifteen minutes. Don't try to shift him." Layla's voice said.

Narla wrapped a jacket around Jaxon's side while Ellie continued to push down on the wound.

"Let me take over." Karson squatted beside her with a piece of shirt material in his hand.

She lifted her hands and blood squirted out for the few seconds it took Karson to replace her hands. He applied pressure until the now blood soaked material appeared to stop the flow.

Ellie stood up and glanced at her bloody hands. Oh hell, she felt terrible and everything around her began to spin. Warm hands grabbed her as Scarlett held her, guided her a few steps and they both sat down.

"I'm okay," Ellie whispered as her head cleared. "It all happened so quickly."

"Yes, but better him than us."

"Annette's doing fine now," Wyatt said to Cinders. "You did a grand job."

Cinders looked up at him across to Annette who smiled and rubbed his ears. He wagged his tail but still remained beside her.

Wyatt picked up the rifle, took out a bullet in the breech that was ready to be fired, removed the clip and leaned the weapon against a tree trunk well away from Jaxon.

"We did everything right," he said and placed an arm around Ellie.

"But lucky the drone appeared," she replied.

THE DRONE MOVED AWAY and almost right on the dot, the red and yellow Life Flight Rescue Helicopter arrived a quarter of an hour later. It hovered above them and a ladder dropped. A crewmember climbed down, introduced himself as Max and immediately tended to Jaxon. Ellie watched as he applied first aid to the victim before rolling him onto a stretcher that had been lowered.

He was strapped in and winched up to the helicopter.

"You're Ellie Parkes, principal of Thomas Road School in Lower Hutt?" Max asked.

Ellie smiled. "Yes, I am but how did you know?"

"I have a niece going to your school." He said her name and Ellie could recall a little girl in the junior school.

"She won some races in our school swimming sports, if I remember."

Max grinned. "That's her. She loves swimming."

He guided the stretcher until it was out of reach and watched as another crew person aboard swung the stretcher into the helicopter and waved to say that all was well.

Max turned to Ellie. "As the victim is your husband, Ellie, we have room for you aboard the helicopter and are allowed to include relations if this situation. Would you like to accompany him to the Wairarapa Hospital in Masterton."

Ellie felt cold. "No," she almost spat as tears filled her eyes "We are separated and he attempted to kill us. There is no way I wish to be with the cowardly man."

Max grimaced. "I'm sorry. I didn't mean to offend you."

"You didn't" Ellie whispered. "Thank you for being kind. If there is room, perhaps you could take Annette back instead. She was a victim in that fire in Hutt City a few weeks back and ..."

"No," Annette cut in. "I want to stay. I'm okay."

Max turned and studied Annette, "Are you sure?" he asked. "There is room aboard, you know?"

Annette shook her head.

"So, how about an injection to relieve the pain in your arm?" Max continued. "It's quite sore, isn't it?"

"A bit," Annette muttered and accepted the help.

"Well," Wyatt said after the helicopter flew away. "We're all safe so I suggest we go back to the ATV unless anyone wants to continue on to Riversdale Beach."

Nobody did so they headed back. With tension gone, everyone chattered and openly expressed how terrified they had been especially after Jaxon had begun shooting at them. The journey back was mainly down hill and it seemed that hardly any time had gone by before they walked down the steps to the ATV. They clamoured aboard. As usual, Cinders found a spot behind everyone's legs at the back and they were off.

BY THE TIME THE ATM reached the remains of the homestead the fire fighters and police had gone but their efforts showed. The homestead was no more. It appeared that nothing survived the intense heat. The dampered down smouldering ruins were still smouldering and too hot to approach. The implement shed was also gone with only skeletal shells of the burnt out Land Cruiser and vintage Ford left.

Wyatt placed his arms around Ellie and nodded down at her. "Shall we go down to the village. I have access to one of the beach cottages. The owners said I can use it any time I wished"

"I guess." Ellie replied. "Oh Wyatt I'm so sorry. This wonderful old house has gone and I somehow feel responsible. If you had not met me it would still be here."

"Don't blame yourself," Wyatt replied and seized her in a hug. "In spite of everything, I am glad we found each other."

"Me too," Ellie responded and cuddled in closer.

WHEN THE LIFE FLIGHT helicopter landed on the helipad beside Wairarapa Hospital a police unit was waiting. The officers closed in and intercepted the stretcher where Jaxon was awake but delirious.

Max stood back and watched. He knew a little about his victim and having someone wanted by the police did happen on occasions. It was just about the end of his shift and the third rescue that day. He checked in, told there were no more call-outs so signed off and headed across to his car in an adjacent carpark.

"Excuse me," said a worried looking woman who was waiting just outside the restricted area. "Can you help me?"

"If I can, Ma'am." Max smiled at her.

"I heard that you just came in from a bush rescue in the ranges south of Riversdale Beach."

"That's true."

"I'm Tara Evans. My daughter, Scarlett and her two companions are stranded in the bush out there somewhere where the news said there was a gunman at large."

Max grinned. "Yeah, that's him on the stretcher but don't you worry for I was talking to Scarlett just a few moments ago. She and the others are fine."

Tara's face lit up but she clapped a hand to her face. "Oh My God, she was involved?"

"Indirectly, I think. Nobody else was hurt in the incident."

"So where is she now?" Tara asked.

"I'll check for you." Max walked across to one of the police officers, spoke for a moment and returned to Tara.

"Scarlett and the others are walking out of the bush to a farm vehicle they have waiting. The police said that they all decided to head back to Wyatt Sigley's homestead."

"But wasn't it burnt down?"

"That's true, Tara. The latest news is that they were going to stay in one of of the beach cottages that Wyatt has access to."

"And how do I get there?"

Max grinned again. Tara sounded like the typical over-protective mother. "It's quite a long way to drive and the road is just a local one. It's windy and narrow."

"Tell me, please," Tara pleaded.

"Sure. If you have a mobile I can set it up on a Google map."

Tara brought out a pink encased mobile and handed it to him. "Thank you," she gasped. "I'm sorry for being such a nuisance."

"No problem. I'm glad I could tell you good news about your daughter. Great kid isn't she?"

Tara smiled. "Well she's a young woman now. Second year at varsity and almost too independent but I guess you know the sort."

"I do. My own kids are at primary school but they grow up so quickly, don't they?"

"Too quickly," Tara sighed. "So confident, too. Sometimes I think she's looking after me and not the other way around."

IT WAS AFTER ELEVEN that evening at the beach cottage. Finally after discussing all their thoughts, having a meal and allowing themselves to relax, it was time for bed after that last cup of coffee.

Cinders, who had been sitting across the room in front of a heater, sat up and growled.

"What is it, Boy?" Wyatt asked.

A faint knock sounded at the outside door off the kitchen.

"I'll get it," Wyatt continued.

With the others all on alert and watching, he turned on the porch light and opened the door. A nervous looking woman stood there.

"Mum!" screamed Scarlett who stood beside Wyatt. "What are you doing here?" She turned to the others. "This is my mum, Tara. Damned if I know how she found us at this late hour."

Tara stepped forward and embraced her daughter before looking around at the others. "Max the helicopter medic said you were all fine but I had to come and see for myself."

"Oh Mum," Scarlett said. "Come in. We're just having a coffee before gong to bed. Want one?"

"If it's not too much trouble," Tara said.

She walked in and grinned. "It was a bit scary driving out here all alone. I didn't pass any cars after I hit the metal road. I saw the remains of the homestead so came back to the village. It was deserted and this was the only place with any lights on. I hoped it would be you all and I was right,

She laughed and glanced around as Scarlett introduced those her mother didn't know.

"Hi," Tara grinned at Cinders. "You even have a lovely dog to protect you."

'That's Cinders," Wyatt said. "He heard you before you even knocked." He scratched the dog's ears. "Tara is a friend, Cinders."

Now reassured, Cinders looked up, wagged his tail and licked Tara's extended hand. Another friend was always welcome.

ELLIE WAS IMPRESSED by Tara. In many ways she could see where Scarlett got her mannerisms and so forth from. Sure, Tara did perhaps treat Scarlett like a teenager but what mothers her age didn't treat adult children that way?

Tara was allocated a bunk in a bunkroom that held eight bunks and had even risen early in the morning and insisted on cooking a breakfast for everyone.

Her arrival too, solved the problem of transport back home. Her Hyundai Santa Fe, a seven seater was a bit of a squeeze with their entire luggage and, of course Cinders but they managed.

By mid morning after everything was packed up and with the ATV tucked in around the back of the cottage, they headed home to Hutt City to let those who lived there off first. Tara lived about fifty kilometres north of Wellington but insisted on dropping Scarlett and her two friends off at their flat in the city itself first,

Everyone promised to stay in touch and probably would, for though half were strangers who had only recently met, a bond between them all had built up. As the Santa Fe drove away with a toot Ellie glanced at Annette and Wyatt.

"Well back to the mundane," she said. "I said I'd be back at school after lunch." She turned to Annette. "And you promised to visit the doctor."

Annette laughed. "Careful Ellie, you're sounding like Tara telling Scarlett what to do."

Ellie grinned. "Guess so but I found Tara wasn't as bad as Scarlett had originally portrayed."

"True," Annette replied. "So true."

CHAPTER 16

Though Jaxon was still a patient in hospital, he was considered fit enough to be escorted the few kilometres to the Masterton District Court for official charges to be laid against him and for his plea to be taken.

After hearing the charges against him and supporting statements on his application for bail the district court judge raised his eyes from a monitor and fixed Jaxon with a stern expression. "I have listened to your attorney's submission, Mr Parkes. However, the charges against you are serious and the police statement that even more charges are imminent, firmly override any arguments that you should be allowed bail.

As well, the Crown Prosecutor's testament that you show little or no remorse and will continue to pursue a vendetta against your estranged wife with little regard to any restrictions imposed by any bail conditions led me to my decision.

Your application is therefore denied. My judgement is that you will remain in custody until your case is brought before the High Court. There may be a long wait but ultimately it will be heard before a jury of your peers, the method that you chose to use."

He shifted his eyes to the corrections officers standing behind Jaxon. "Escort Mr Parkes back to hospital where on discharge he will be transferred to Rimutaka Remand Prison to await trial in the High Court at a date yet to be established."

"Bastard," Jaxon muttered under his breath and glanced up at the spectators, hoping to see Ellie.

But she was not there. There was nobody there that he knew, only strangers and reporters who showed no remorse at all about his plight.

Why had the world turned against him?

WYATT WAS IN HIS OFFICE when Cynthia walked in with a pout on her face.

"Okay, what is it?" he asked his secretary.

She shut the door, something she never did. "I tried to put her off but she is insistent about seeing you. I said I'd check to see if you were still here as you could be out with a client." She sort of shrugged. "I can tell her you're not here, if you wish."

"Who?" Wyatt asked.

"Jennifer your ex."

Wyatt frowned. His contacts with Jennifer had always been through their lawyers. If he refused to see her, no doubt another legal claim would be made that would cost a small fortune to defend. Her claim for half of any insurance money from the homestead fire had already been lodged. His own lawyer suggestion that an out of court settlement would save thousands of dollars of legal fees was one he was considering.

"Send her in," he said. "Leave the intercom on though and record everything she has to say."

Jennifer looked older than he remembered but this could be because she was dressed in casual clothes of a top and jeans without any make up. She also looked nervous rather than aggressive as she just stood there holding her handbag.

"Hello Jennifer," Wyatt said in a neutral voice. He walked out from behind his desk, guided her to an armchair and sat in a second one. "I hope you recovered from your ordeal and are on the mend."

She shrugged "I was terrified, Wyatt but I am okay now. It made me think about everything." She glanced up and looked at him. "I know we are divorced but do we need to be enemies a well?"

Wyatt frowned. He studied her as his mind reached back. For a decade they had been quite happily married before everything had gradually turned sour. But could she be trusted? Too many years of antagonism had gone by and her claims since they had separated were still unsettled.

"No of course not but I have attempted to be reasonable, you know."

"I know," Jennifer replied.

He stared. This was the first time in years that she had ever admitted that fact.

"So why are you here?"

Jennifer reached into her handbag, took out a letter and handed it to him.

Wyatt unfolded the letter inside and read it. The letter was from her lawyer and advised her that in his professional opinion, any further claims against Wyatt had only a slim chance of success. Furthermore any counter-claim for court expenses could amount to over $25,000. If the case was lost and it probably would be, this would be added to any amount she owed.

Jennifer handed Wyatt a second letter. In it was a statement from her lawyer for $12,000.

"I can't even pay his bill?" Jennifer said. "I've no money."

"None?" gasped Wyatt. "When we separated, you received half of everything except my inheritance from my grandmother that your claims have been all about. What you did receive was enough to keep you well off financially for years. What happened?"

"Finlay Gower ripped me off," she whispered.

Finlay was Jennifer's partner who had been largely responsible for their marriage breakup in the first place. As far as Wyatt knew, they had been together ever since she had left him. He had assumed they had married but had never queried Jennifer's continued use of his surname, Sigley.

"We never actually married," Jennifer said with a shrug. "Who bothers in this day and age?"

"So all your money and assets such as the house were discretely placed in his name?" he asked.

"Not really. I still kept my own bank accounts but he had access to them. You know that when we were married I trusted you for everything to do with finance?"

Wyatt nodded.

"I guess I switched that responsibility to Finlay."

"I see and no doubt he was the one pushing you to claim half my inheritance from Grandma?"

"Yes. In hindsight I can see how he manipulated me for months. He could be very convincing, you know."

"And your latest claims against the homestead?"

"My fault," Jennifer whispered. "By this time Finlay had moved on and I had put my trust in my lawyer."

"Expensive choice," Wyatt said and handed the letters back to her.

Jennifer stared at him. "If I withdraw all claims from your inheritance including any claims for half the value of the homestead, will you help me get out of debt?"

"And the alternative?"

"I'll be declared bankrupt. My bank is about to start proceedings. "

"And any claims against Finlay?"

"He's gone, having also embezzled Leah, the woman he took off to Australia with."

"No doubt a young woman in her twenties who has filthy rich parents?"

"That's about right. I actually feel sorry for her. The last we have both heard from him is that he'd moved to Canada with yet another young woman."

"Pleasant guy." Wyatt barely held back his sarcasm as he stood up. "I need to really think about this, Jennifer. Also I wish to consult my partner about anything that we should agree to do."

"Ellie Parkes, that popular principal at Thomas Road School and ex wife of that psychopath Jaxon Parkes."

"I guess he is. You were lucky that he never killed you."

Jennifer almost smiled. "Yeah, at the time I thought you would be proud of how I escaped from his clutches."

"After all these years?"

Jennifer stared at him and wiped tears from her eyes. "Stupid, wasn't I?"

"Not at all," Wyatt whispered and for a moment was at a loss at what to say. "Thank you for visiting. It took courage to do that. If you give me your mobile number I'll get back to you."

Jennifer rummaged in her purse and handed him a small business card with her name and number but nothing else on it. Suddenly all formal, she held out her hand that he shook, thanked him for his time and left him standing there.

Cynthia appeared. "For what it's worth, I think everything Jennifer said was genuine. I also agree that it took courage for her to swallow her pride and visit you in person."

"Me too, but what shall I tell Ellie?"

"Everything, Wyatt. She's a mature woman. Just be a little careful with Jennifer, though and don't be too generous."

"I guess that's what Ellie would say."

ELLIE SAT IN HER OFFICE with Wyatt and listened to the recording of whole conversation between Jennifer and himself. "Okay,

I don't know her, of course but she did sound as if she needs someone to lean on rather than solving her own problems."

Wyatt nodded. "She has no close relatives and I've no idea whether she has kept any close friends. There were a couple of old high school friends she had when we were married but I have no idea if they're still around."

"Has she a job?" Ellie asked.

Wyatt shrugged. "I have no idea. When we were married she worked as a secretary with a small firm in Wellington but that was years ago."

"And the house you owned when you were married?"

"In our separation agreement she bought me out of my half. There wasn't a lot in it after the mortgage and so forth. As far as I know she still she lives there."

"So we find it all out," Ellie said. "You are not responsible for her, Wyatt. Any final agreement you make needs to be a once and final document with her withdrawing any claims on a share of the homestead insurance."

Wyatt smiled. "Exactly my thoughts. But switching topics, I want you to meet a lady. Will you be free about four?"

"Of course but why does this sound mysterious?"

"It's just easier to show you than just talk about it."

"And the lady?"

"She's a charming elderly lady at a local retirement village."

ELLIE'S VISION OF A huge four-storey retirement village that she had seen in newspaper ads was wrong. Wyatt drove into an almost brand new cluster of villas built in a circle of roads that also contained a large community building.

"Barbara is over ninety but is not what you think," Wyatt said.

He pulled in beside a garage attached to a villa where a woman was washing a small modern car.

"Hi Wyatt," the lady called out. "Your car could do with a wash too, I see."

"Come and meet Barbara," Wyatt said to Ellie.

Ellie's mental vision of a trembling old lady with a walker was as incorrect as her earlier assumption. Barbara looked about sixty as she reached down and turned off a hose tap. She turned and held a hand out to her.

"Hi Ellie. I've heard so much about you. How's Thomas Road School going?" She chuckled. "But come in. I'll put the kettle on. Want a cup of coffee?"

"I'd love one thanks," Ellie replied and walked into a modern open-space kitchen and living area. On Barbara's invitation she sat behind a breakfast nook.

"Barbara was a teacher too," Wyatt said.

"A long time ago," Barbara continued. "In my day all the principals were men but women did the hard work. I was an infant mistress, as they called them then, at Hutt Central. I remember when Thomas Road School was opened. That would be in the eighties..." She chattered on and brought out a tray of scones from the oven and began spreading jam on half a dozen.

"Do you like the village?" Ellie asked when she could get a word in.

Barbara smiled. "I didn't think I would but actually love it here. If it wasn't for my two daughters giving me a nudge I'd still be in the homestead." She laughed. 'That's what we call our place even though our farm around it had been sold. But that is why you're here isn't it?"

Ellie caught Wyatt's eyes and raised her eyebrows when he smiled at her. "I'd love to see it, Barbara," she said.

ACROSS THE MOTORWAY to the west of the city, steep hills rose with a forested area with flora similar to that around McArthur's Hutt. Over the years valleys in the area became suburbs for the city below while the more rugged land remained a part of Belmont Regional Park with only a few winding roads through forested land.

Ellie sat in the rear seat with Cinders beside her so Barbara could be at the front to help navigate for Wyatt. They turned off up a narrow road called Taylor's Road and after about a kilometre, arrived in a small area where the valley widened out and the bush turned into farmland.

Barbara turned to talk to Ellie. "My maiden name was Taylor and the farm we going by right now was owned by my great grandparents. It was subdivided and sold off after the Second World War but my father kept one farm that I later inherited. My family's story is a little like what Wyatt told me about his. I lived here as a child but became a teacher and moved away. My brother ran the family farm that we had shared ownership of. To cut a long story short I moved back here with my husband who was a farmer while I taught at various schools in Hutt Valley.

When both my brother, who never married and my husband died within two months of each other about two decades ago I sold the farm but kept the homestead and a few surrounding paddocks. Except for my present move I've lived there ever since."

Wyatt slowed and drove around a corner where a Victorian homestead appeared. It was a little smaller than Wyatt's homestead but had two storeys, was painted white and was surrounded by a lawn and well-kept flower gardens.

"Apart from a couple of casual tenants it's been empty since I left but I have a contractor who mows the lawn and tends to the gardens," Barbara said as they pulled up by the back door. "The interior needs renovation but I had the exterior repainted about three years back."

"I was thinking of using the homestead insurance and buying it rather than rebuilding out at Greystone Beach. It depends on the outcome of any agreement with Jennifer and you, of course," Wyatt said.

"Me?" gasped Ellie.

Wyatt looked embarrassed. "I might need an input from you. Barbara is very generous but she does have two married daughters, four grandchildren and a great grandson to think of."

"There is no hurry," Barbara cut in. "I told Wyatt I will give him the first option for three months." She shrugged. "Daughters can be bossy at times."

"And no doubt they're thinking of you," Ellie responded.

"Possibly," Barbara said with a sigh. "That's the situation at the moment. Anyway, welcome to Taylor's View Homestead."

She waved out to where in a gap between two hills; Ellie could see Hutt River, the motorway, railway line and the city beyond.

"What a wonderful view," she gasped.

"There wasn't much there when Great Grandad arrived." Barbara replied. "I often thought I should write a book about the area. It has a rich history going back hundreds of years, even before Europeans arrived."

"So do it." Ellie opened the door and Cinder's bounded out to start his sniffing quest before catching up with them at a side door with his tail wagging.

"Let him come in," Barbara said. "We always allowed our dogs in for they were pets and not just working dogs."

The house had that usual musty smell from being locked up but was clean and tidy. Ellie noticed that the kitchen, bathroom and bedrooms were in need of modernisation but were completely liveable. Wyatt seemed to be deep in thought but they both made positive comments about everything. Barbara was obviously proud of her home and often told little things about her life there through the years.

After almost an hour they left and drove Barbara home after insisting on taking her to a coffee bar for a late coffee. She chatted away and appeared to appreciate her time with them.

AFTER THEY LEFT HER with a promise to get back they bought takeaways and returned to Ellie's place.

"So what did you think of it?" he asked as they munched their meal.

"I liked it and found Barbara a fine old lady. There is much to consider, though."

Wyatt nodded. "There are a few points I'd like to make, too. First, to avoid any complaints from other purchasers I withdrew from being Barbara's real estate agent and recommended that she should approach another company. "

"Would there be any others wanting to buy it?"

"Plenty but it is too expensive for most," Wyatt replied. "Two developers want to rip the house down and build a new subdivision on the land. She still owns eight hectares of the land around the homestead, which is about twenty acres in the old measurement. This is enough to create quite a large subdivision of high priced places with that view of the city." He grimaced. "When I was handling the sale she would have nothing to do with that and insisted on a covenant that prevented any purchaser from pulling the house down or sub-dividing the land for twenty years."

"And that still applies?"

"Yes, it is all legal and the new real-estate agent knows about it."

"And that affects the price?"

"Oh yes. With the two companies competing Barbara could get over a hundred thousand more than the present asking price."

"I see and the other bit?"

Wyatt stared at her. "You mean shifting in together and making it a partnership?'"

Ellie flushed. "Something like that."

"Legally, it won't be hard to make up a partnership so we own half each or any other percentage depending on how much you want to invest..."

"Damn the legality of it Wyatt. I'm talking about us. We have both moved on from marriages that failed and are both professional people." She gulped. "I think we are, or were, both lonely and therefore vulnerable. "

Wyatt's face dropped. "So you don't want to do this?"

Ellie stared at him and her chin shook. "Did I say that?"

"No."

Ellie continued speaking. "We've got that three months Barbara offered us. I just think we should take that time to consider everything. This can include whether you should rebuild your homestead or accept a cash offer from the insurance company and sell the bare land there." She sighed. "There is also Jennifer to consider. We still have no watertight agreement over any settlement she may agree to. If she continues to demand half the homestead's value, court cases could drag out for years. "

"Okay," Wyatt grinned. "You summed up my thoughts completely. I can see why Thomas Road is such a sort after school in the city."

Ellie pushed back her empty plate and smiled. "Want some ice cream for desert?" she asked.

ELLIE SPENT MUCH OF the early morning thinking about Barbara's home at Taylor's View. It was certainly a grant old place and she knew that Wyatt would enjoy upgrading the interior. However, it was a valuable property and the asking price was high. Also that covenant that Barbara included meant that if they purchased it they could not sub-divide the land to recuperate some of the cost.

She understood her reasons and agreed that developers with plenty of capital shouldn't be allowed to just pull the homestead down and wipe out her family's history for ever. This, however, did restrict them.

There was also Wyatt and his circumstances to consider. In her opinion he was almost too kind and considerate. This was complete contrast to Jaxon and perhaps why she had fallen in love with him. This was really the first time she had thought of their relationship in that way.

She grimaced as she looked out her office window to where the caretaker was mowing the lawn. Damn the man... the one mowing the lawn, not Wyatt. Why did he have to mow it at nine-thirty in the morning in front of a classroom block at the most valuable teaching time of the day? She was about go out and ask him to do it later but stopped. John was a caring old guy who would do anything for the staff, Board of Trustees or herself. She knew he never mowed lawns at recess times or when teachers were taking classes outside for any reason. Also, with the recent rain and warmer weather the grass had begun to grow quickly and he had a large area of lawn to mow around the school grounds.

From his point of view, this was the logical time to mow and the mower actually had a quiet motor and this lawn would only take about twenty minutes to cut.

She noticed that John had turned the mower around. He glanced up, saw her at the window and gave her a wave. She smiled, waved back and returned to her desk. There was yet another form to complete for the Ministry of Education.

CHAPTER 17

The interview room at the remand prison was austere but not unpleasant. High widows hid any outside view but beneath them the wall displayed a pleasant beach scene painted in pastel colours. In many ways Jaxon thought that this was similar to Greystone Beach and made him relax a little.

He glanced across at Stanley Kendrick, his lawyer who had briefed him up on what to say, what comments to avoid and how to maintain his cool. Flying into a rage would no help his case and would merely play into the police and crown prosecutor's hands. As far as his lawyer and himself knew, the cases against him were all circumstantial so his account of what happened not only affected the charge of arson against him for destroying Wyatt Sigley's homestead but also that of the apartment fire.

He had not been charged with that to date but Kendrick told him in blunt terms that the police were building up a convincing case against him. If they could prove he set the homestead on fire it made his defence of more serious crimes that much harder.

Detective Sergeant Layla Fraser and the constable, Jaxon had forgotten his name, walked into the room and sat behind a table facing Stanley and himself.

"We shall get started," Sergeant Fraser continued with the usual preamble about the time and so forth before she glanced at the iPad she held flicked through several pages of notes before staring directly into his eyes. "Before this interview your barrister stated that you have a statement to make. Is that correct?"

Jaxon gulped. "Yes. I admit being at the scene and confronting Mrs Jennifer Sigley at the fire of her homestead but I did not start the fire." He glanced at Stanley who gave a slight nod of encouragement. "I arrived at Greystone Beach as I wanted to speak to my wife Ellie who I believed was staying at the homestead."

"Why?" spat the sergeant.

"I wanted to save our marriage," Jaxon said. "We were going through a rough patch in our relationship but I was sure we could solve our differences."

He expected her to bring up that he had assaulted Ellie and was ready to defend his actions but Fraser just glanced at him and nodded. "So where at Greystone Beach were you?" she asked instead.

"The motor camp, I saw that the homestead was on fire so went to investigate."

"The camping ground is over a kilometre away from the homestead," the constable said. "There was no way you could see the building from there could you?"

Jaxon felt his temper rise in his throat as he clenched his fists but managed to swallow his pride. "Of course I couldn't see it," he said. "However, the sky was lit up in that direction and I knew there was fire. The homestead was the only building in that direction."

"Fair enough," Fraser said. "So what happened when you arrived on your motorbike?"

"The rear of the building was ablaze and I saw this woman carrying a petrol can running out across the lawn away from the building. She saw me and ran for a car parked nearby."

"What sort of car?" the constable asked.

Jaxon shrugged. "I don't know, one of those flash German brands, I think."

"Go on," Fraser continued.

"I confronted and tried to stop her but she was already in the car. She swung it around and purposely attempted to run me down. Luckily I jumped aside and managed to avoid being hit. She took off and I followed." Jaxon continued on with his description of the chase and what happened at the river when he saw the police vehicle there.

Fraser held up a hand. "Why did you have a rifle?" she asked.

"It's my hunting rifle," Jaxon replied. "I took it with me as I didn't know what to expect when I got to the homestead."

"And you confronted Mrs Jennifer Sigley with it?" the constable cut in.

"Not really. I may have held it up when she tried to run me down."

"And fired it at the car destroying the rear window?"

"Possibly. I wanted to shoot out the tyres."

"Oh come now," scoffed the constable. "You're a hunter who knows how to fire a rifle. "Tyres are a long way below a car's back window."

"The car was accelerating away and going downhill."

"So you followed her to the river and saw her crash the car near the police vehicle?" Fraser asked.

"Yes."

"So why didn't you just go across to the police and tell them what you just told us?"

"I was panicking, I guess." Jaxon retorted almost forgetting to remain calm. "I still held the rifle and knew they would not believe me."

"Interesting," Sergeant Layla Fraser said. "That is all the questioning today, Mr Parkes. This interview is over,"

"Is that everything?" Stanley asked

"At the moment, yes."

The sergeant stood up, nodded the constable and they both walked out of the room.

Stanley frowned and looked up at the nearby guard. "I need to speak to my client in confidence about this interview," he said and nodded at the one-way mirror along the opposite wall "Where can we do this?"

"You can go to a holding cell," the guard replied and turned to a second guard by the door. "Take Parkes and his lawyer to one," he ordered.

"IT'S ALL LIES," ZACK said as they drove back to the police station. "Though I must admit, he controlled himself more than during earlier interviews."

"Stanley Kendrick is one of the city's top barristers and advised him against becoming angry. It almost worked," Layla replied

"So you saw him clench his fists?"

"Oh I did and also when he lied he sort of looked over my shoulder and couldn't make eye contact. That was a dead give away."

"But not enough to convince any jury?"

"True. However, we still need to follow up his accusations. It's a pity that Jennifer Sigley was there. A neutral eyewitness nothing to do with Wyatt would have been more helpful. We're still looking for someone and will check with the manager at the South Pacific View Station. Workers there were the only ones in the area at that time?"

"And the murder or man slaughter charges relating him to the apartment building?"

"It's coming on well but there is no urgency. Having him in custody on remand helps. We need to make everything watertight." Layla glanced at the constable. "That's going to be part of your job, Zack. Think you can handle it?"

"I can try, Layla." he replied. "Annette Patterson is a reliable person who can be a great help if we can prove Jaxon mistook her for Ellie."

"Good. Meanwhile, I'll have more words with Jennifer Sigley. At the moment it is a case of her words against Jaxon Parkes. However, she certainly seems to have a vendetta against Wyatt that Jaxon's lawyer will pounce upon."

ELLIE HAD BEEN INVITED to Kerenza's classroom to see a presentation that concluded a language and social studies unit the class had been doing. It was well done with wonderful artwork and an accompanying spoken and musical presentation. It had just concluded and she was telling the class how wonderful it was when she felt her iPhone vibrate.

She stopped, excused herself and stepped away to answer it.

"Thomas Road School, Ellie Parkes speaking," she said.

"My, how formal," replied Wyatt's voice. "Sorry to interrupt something important."

She smiled. "It is but I know you wouldn't call unless it was urgent."

"It could be. Jennifer just called and she's in one hell of a state, all sobs and almost incoherent."

Ellie felt slightly annoyed. "Give me ten minutes and I'll call you back. Okay?"

"Sure," he said.

She apologised to the class and continued with her praise. Kerenza beamed and the class clapped when she had finished.

"But I must leave you. I am proud of you all, every one of you," she said and smiled at Camden, a little mainstreamed boy who had come along way during the year under Kerenza's care. He caught her eyes, something he couldn't do earlier in the year and a grin spread over his face.

"Bye," she said and waved back at the children's waves as she left the room.

Out in the quadrangle she called Wyatt back as she headed towards her office.

"Sorry," she said. "I've just seen a wonderful presentation and wanted to thank the children."

"Kerenza's class wasn't it?"

"You remembered?"

"Of course. I had forgotten the time, though."

"Oh Wyatt, I know I rattle on about school and must bore you."

"You don't. Did Camden start screaming?"

"You remembered him, too? No, he hardly ever does now. He was perfect and even did a tiny part." Ellie grinned. "But tell me about Jennifer."

"She reckons they're going to charge her with arson for setting fire to the homestead. Could you come around to my place this evening just before six? I persuaded her I wouldn't be home until then." He coughed as if embarrassed. "I think I'd like your support to deal with her."

"Won't I just antagonise her?"

"I doubt it. She knows about us. It seems that she found out all about you and your reputation at Thomas Road School. Your high reputation has spread."

"I guess she never heard from the moaners. Yes, I'll be there, all prim and proper."

Wyatt laughed. "No, the real you will be sufficient," he replied.

Ellie smiled as she clicked off. Wyatt had that knack of making her feel appreciated.

ELLIE ARRIVED AT WYATT'S place about quarter to six after driving home and changing into a casual top and jeans. She really had no idea what Jennifer would be like and told herself not to prejudge the woman.

Just after six a car arrived in the driveway behind her car and a woman, presumably Jennifer, got out and walked to towards the house.

The doorbell rang and Wyatt indicated that he wanted her beside him when he opened the door. She grimaced but stood beside him.

"Hi Jennifer," Wyatt said. "Come on in and meet Ellie Parkes, my partner."

Ellie noticed the brunette woman who was about her own age. She wore a modern skirt and sweater, low heeled shoes and had little or no make upon. Her face looked stressed and nervous as she squeezed a handkerchief in her hand.

"Hello Jennifer," she said.

Jennifer looked at her, stepped forward, burst into tears and fling her arms around her neck like some long lost friend. Ellie just held her and glanced over her shoulder at Wyatt who looked almost as embarrassed as she felt.

Jennifer clung to her for a moment before she stepped back and apologised. She wiped her eyes and smiled slightly. "Sorry," she said. "I could hardly hug my divorced husband, now could I?"

"Why not?" Wyatt replied. He stepped forward and gave her a brief hug. "But come in. Would you like a coffee or perhaps a wine?"

"A coffee will be fine. White, one sugar. As you may remember wine just goes straight to my head. "

"I'll get it," Ellie said, relieved to be doing something in the strange situation.

Moments later, Jennifer sat in an armchair sipping her coffee and munching a muffin. She looked at her in the eyes "I've heard about you, Ellie," she said. "Building up a run-down school that parents avoided to one the in-crowd wants to have their kids at is quite an achievement."

"Thank you Jennifer. It's all teamwork but not just me, you know."

"So tell us everything that happened with the police," Wyatt cut in.

"Oh they were pleasant enough when they arrived at my place and asked if I could accompany them back to the police station to answer a few questions about the events at our homestead." Jennifer placed her coffee on a nearby table, wiped her eyes again and continued to talk...

"SO YOU HAVE EXPLAINED everything about your ongoing claim for half the value of the homestead that your ex-husband inherited after your separation and subsequent divorce, Jennifer," Detective Sergeant Layla Fraser said in a stern voice.

"It was before our marriage broke up," Jennifer replied.

"Whatever," Layla replied. "Your claims on the property are not my concern but the reason why you were there on that particular day is. Can you enlighten me?"

"I knew Wyatt was visiting the homestead that weekend and wanted to speak to him about my claim." Jennifer's hands shook as she glanced up from downcast eyes. "My lawyer seemed to be getting nowhere and suggested that a court case was the only way to settle an impasse. Even he admitted that the cost could be prohibitive and the wait for a civil case to be heard would be at least a couple of years."

"So you decided to take the matter into your own hands?"

"I just wanted to talk to Wyatt about it."

"You also heard he had a new girlfriend, a respected principal in town and were jealous in spit of you both being separated for almost a decade?"

Jennifer squirmed in her seat. "No, that had nothing to do with it."

The detective glowered. "Or perhaps what motivated you most was that your most recent partner left you taking most of your money. He absconded for Australia and you lost contact with him so decided to tackle Wyatt Sigley for more money?"

"Of course not."

Layla clicked on her iPad and read something to herself from the screen. "I see you changed your surname back to Sigley from Whitman by deed poll last year." She looked up. "Now why was that?"

"I didn't want to keep the surname of the man who swindled me out of my life savings."

"So it wasn't just to support your claim for half the homestead inheritance you believed you are entitled to have?"

Questions on just about everything on her adult life continued. The police knew just about everything about her, especially her life since leaving Wyatt, her affairs, other casual encounters and the several jobs she had had over a decade.

"So you found out about Ellie Parkes and her problems with a violent Jaxon Parkes. This gave you a perfect victim to blame for torching the homestead?" Detective Sergeant Layla Fraser accused. "With the building destroyed you could therefore claim half the insurance payout and your financial worries would be over?"

"No!" Jennifer burst into tears. "Everything I told you was true. Jaxon Parkes held me up at gunpoint and even taunted me about being blamed for starting the fire. I was terrified and thought he was about to rape me."

"But he didn't!"

"No. I managed to get away and was rescued by the police. You know he shot out the back window of my car." She sobbed.

Layla Fraser's voice softened. "I do know all about that, Jennifer, I realise you were terrified and if the police were not at the river the outcome could have been far more serious than they were." She stood up. "You can go. Thank you for helping us in our inquiries. An officer will drive you home."

"And that's it?" Jennifer gasped.

"For the moment, yes. However, we may need to speak to you again."

JENNIFER SIPPED THE last of her coffee and glanced at Wyatt and Ellie. "That's the situation at the moment but I needed you, both of you to understand what happened. I had nothing to do with the fire. Jaxon Parkes did it so why do they blame me?"

"I don't know," Wyatt said in a kind voice. "However, I shall find out why. It certainly sounds like police harassment to me."

"I think Jaxon made that accusation and they had to check it out," Ellie added. "He's an expert in blaming others to defend himself. I'm sure the police realise that."

"But did they have to be so horrible about it?" Jennifer whispered.

ACROSS THE CITY AT the police laboratories Doctor Ian Dempsey waited as Layla studied a selection of named fragments on a bench.

"Article 37 is a significant find, Layla," he said.

In a sealed plastic bag was a screw top. She picked the bag up and examined it. To her it looked like any other top used to screw on a container. The main difference she noted was that it was metal rather than plastic.

"This was found in our recent search around the Sigley Homestead site. It had been tossed away and wasn't found in our initial search. It's the screw top for a petrol can."

"One that could have been used to douse petrol on the building?"

"Exactly," Ian replied and nodded at a petrol can on a side bench. This is a common brand sold in town. The top fits this can perfectly."

"But there is more?" Layla asked.

Ian grinned. "Yes, as I said it was tossed into the grass and actually escaped the flames." He grinned. "I lifted a perfect thumb and finger print from it and guess whose they were?"

Layla grinned. "Jaxon Parkes?"

"You're spot on. Now what innocent reason would he be there for unscrewing a petrol can if it wasn't to set the building alight? We have already established that an accelerant was used along the rear of the homestead to start the fire."

"Got yah!" Layla gasped. "Thanks Ian. This is just what we need to nail the bastard."

"And let Jennifer Sigley off?"

Layla nodded. "I never really thought she was responsible but had to check out Jaxon Parkes' accusation. We had already found that she was trying to claim half the value of the homestead not covered in their divorce settlement. That was enough to warrant an investigation. I guess she was just at the wrong place at the wrong time."

She reached out and shook Ian's hand. "Now, all we need is to link him in with that apartment fire in High Street."

"I might be able to help you with that, too. His fingerprints were found there as well. Tell me, is he an arrogant type of guy?"

"He is. Why?"

"Both times he never bothered to wear gloves. Even the most useless petty thief knows about fingerprints."

"I'll give Jennifer a call tomorrow and let her off the hook. I guess I was a bit harsh on her in the interview."

"It's called being thorough," Ian replied.

CHAPTER 18

Ellie continued to enjoy having Annette as a flat mate in her apartment. For the third time there had been a delay in Annette's new apartment at *Hillview Apartments.* It was something to do with the whole block having to be strengthened after the fire. The latest news was that it wouldn't be ready until early in the new year.

It was a wet miserable Saturday, Wyatt was at work as he usually was with open homes to display to prospective purchasers and Annette had volunteered to look over the separation and divorce agreements between him and Jennifer.

"The trouble is that I like Jennifer," Ellie said. "She is not the vindictive person I imagined before I met her. Sure she has had a few flings since leaving Wyatt and she was certainly ripped off by that last guy who swindled her from practically everything."

"I may be able to help with that," Annette produced a file from those piled on the table. "Didn't she say she lived with the guy for two years before he left the country and emptied her bank accounts?"

"I think so."

"This is significant for in New Zealand a de facto relationship is not legally recognised until the couple have been living together for at least three years. Didn't she also tell you her bank account was in her name and not a joint account?"

"Yes, but he had access to them and just withdrew all her money."

"That wasn't legally his."

"I see but he has left the country and can't be traced."

"No but her bank failed to protect her money. With huge amounts being withdrawn they should have checked with her before allowing the withdrawals. Did they do it?"

Ellie shrugged. "I have no idea. Shall I call and ask her?"

Annette nodded. "Perhaps if she could come around it could help. There's another thing I need to discuss with her, too."

Jennifer arrived half an hour later and grinned at Annette when they were introduced. "I thought Ellie was shacked up with Wyatt," she said but with a twinkle in her eye.

"Not yet," Ellie replied. "Annette also had a rough experience with Jaxon..." She gave a brief account of the fire at *Hillview Apartment*s before continuing. "Annette is a partner in a Wellington law firm and thinks she can help you recover some, if not all of your money that guy swindled from you."

"You can?" Jennifer gasped. "I was told by the police that he had left the country and couldn't be traced."

"Not him," Annette explained. "I suggest that you get your lawyer to claim your money back from the bank for they failed to protect it for you." She repeated what she had earlier told Ellie.

"Oh my God!" Jennifer whispered. "As a lawyer, can you do it for me?"

"It will be fine as long as Ellie doesn't require me in that capacity. You would have to go through my firm but can nominate me as your personal lawyer. However, we cannot represent you both as there could be a conflict of interest."

"No, go ahead," Ellie replied. "I've had my own lawyer for years and he does a reasonably good job."

"You will need to tell me everything about your money, your bank accounts and how you found out it was missing. Also, I'll need dates in relation of your de facto relationship with the man..."

"Finlay Gower," Jennifer added.

Jennifer wrote his name down and continued on. "As your lawyer, there is one other item I need to advise you on."

Jennifer frowned. "And that is..."

"I will need to legally go into it but my opinion is that any claims you make against Wyatt for half the value of his homestead will not succeed. It is all to do with the heirloom inheritance in our law. That is, something valuable that has been passed down through the generations. In our law this is not included in the division of property in any separation or divorce procedures."

"Okay but back to my bank accounts, you think you have a good chance of the bank being required to refund me my savings?" Jennifer asked.

"Oh yes. They do not like any publicity if we go to the next step and approach the banking ombudsman."

"I see, but as my lawyer you don't recommend I continue the claim on half the insurance payout on Wyatt's homestead?"

"I do but the decision must be yours. I can only advise you."

Jennifer turned to Ellie. "And what do you think, Ellie?"

"What I think doesn't really matter for I am a third party and am not legally involved."

"But it does to me," Jennifer replied.

"Of course I would prefer that withdraw your claim. However, I suggest you think about it and await any outcome from getting the bank to restore your money."

"If it is restored, the bank would also be obliged to withdraw the bankrupt procedure against you," Annette said. "Any amounts owed on your mortgage can be deducted from the net total you receive back into your accounts. I assume you will have sufficient funds to cover this?"

"Oh yes. Most of my settlement from Wyatt's and my divorce was still in a term deposit that Finlay accessed." Jennifer said. "If I get it back I won't want any more from Wyatt or the homestead payout."

"Right," Annette said. "I'll make you an appointment to come in next week and we'll set everything up legally."

"Can it be on Monday?" Jennifer asked in an excited voice.

"Sure but will take a while for everything to happen. Anything legal takes time."

ANNETTE WAS NOT THE slightest bit intimidated by the general manager of TasmanBlue Bank, a local bank named after the ocean between New Zealand and Australia that, in turn, was named after the first European explorer who 'discovered' both lands. The firm's headquarters were in Wellington.

"I can only allow you ten minutes to state your case, Ms Patterson," he said in a cold voice.

"Allow me, Mr Meyer!" she retorted and stared him directly in the eyes. "You are in no position to allow or disallow me anything. You are the general manager of this bank and are obliged to hear out my concerns about how one of your customers has been mistreated. If you wish to maintain a hierarchy you are answerable to me not vice versa. If you refuse to hear of my concerns, my next appointment shall be with the banking ombudsman who I have learnt, is already following up several other similar complaints by your company since you became general manager."

Myers looked away. "I have followed up reports from the manager of our Hutt City branch and find they did everything correctly with Mrs Sigley's accounts. Before the three large withdrawals by her partner of the time were allowed she was contacted and agreed to every withdrawal."

"By email, Mr Meyer? All Finlay Gower had to do was sit in front of the computer and pretend he was her. How secure is that? The very least your manager should have met her in person so she could verify the withdrawals."

"With all the large withdrawals we handle in a day, this is physically impossible to do."

"Furthermore," Annette continued ignoring his response. "By law, de facto relationships are not recognised in our country unless the parties concerned have been living together for three years. Jennifer Sigley and Finlay Gower were living together for one week over two years so he had no legal right to access her accounts."

"We did not know that they were together for less than the required legal time." His voice sounded less authoritative.

"Ignorance of any law is no excuse."

"Very well, I shall listen to your concern about Mrs Sigley's accounts; I believe there were three."

"Yes. The worse is that of a long-term investment that was not due to expire until next year ..." She continued on with a detailed account of everything that had happened. This included how Jennifer had originally contacted their bank and followed this up by going to the police and the subsequent follow up."

She glanced at her watch before she continued and noticed she had been in the office for forty minutes. "My firm has found that your bank has failed to protect Jennifer's accounts and she should be reimbursed the full amount of the illegal withdrawals."

She took out a document several pages thick from her satchel and placed it on his desk. "The full details are in this document."

"You are thorough," Meyer's admitted as he slowly turned the pages over.

"I have to be," Annette replied and produced a second document. "This one is about the withdrawal of any bankrupt proceedings against her." She eyeballed him again. "You have ten days to reply to our requests. Of course, you may seek legal advice from your own lawyers if that is your wish."

She stood up and held out her hand that he shook. "Good afternoon to you, Mr Myers. I too, am a busy person with much to do today."

She turned and left without a backward glance.

BY THURSDAY ANOTHER busy week was almost over. Annette and Ellie were having their evening meal when there was a tap on the door.

"Expecting anyone?" Annette asked for the only casual visitor was Wyatt who would just walk in after calling out that he had arrived.

"No." Ellie walked across and opened the door.

"Hi Ellie," said a beaming Jennifer. "Is Annette here?"

What a contrast there was compared to their original meeting. Jennifer was dressed in a comfortable looking business suit with slacks rather than a skirt.

"I'm here, Jennifer," Annette called out from across the room. "Come in. I guess the bank contacted you."

"Did they what!" Jennifer tore across the room waving a bank statement. "They've done everything including giving me a hundred dollar Visa Gift Card for the stress they caused... " She continued on to say that all her accounts were restored to their full net amount before Finlay began the withdrawals. Amounts to cover the missed mortgage payments and other automatic payments such as the power bill were deducted from her main account and interest had been added onto her long-term deposit one.

"You did this didn't you, Annette?" Jennifer almost shouted and gave her a hug.

"We managed to persuade the TasmanBlue Bank that they did not protect your accounts adequately." Annette said modestly.

Ellie interrupted. "She did more than that. Annette went straight to the general manager at their head office in Wellington and told him in no uncertain terms what the legal consequences would be if he didn't reinstate your accounts and withdraw the bankruptcy threat."

Jennifer turned to Annette, "You didn't?"

Ellie frowned slightly. "And now comes your part of our bargain?"

Jennifer looked puzzled. "And that is?"

"The withdrawal of any claims you have for half of Wyatt's insurance payout for his homestead at Greystone Beach."

Jennifer shrugged. "Oh that! It has already been done. I have legally withdrawn any claims I had on the homestead. Didn't Annette tell you?"

Ellie turned to her friend and raised her eyebrows.

"I was going to wait until Wyatt was with you," Annette said. "Jennifer did it yesterday after I told her that the long term account claim to the bank had succeeded. At that time, I didn't know how successful the other two accounts would be for the small print in them about liability is different."

"And you never told us?" Ellie gasped.

"Well it didn't legally come through until this afternoon."

"Meanie," Ellie gasped but burst into a smile.

ON SATURDAY AFTERNOON, even the weather seemed to shine over Ellie, Wyatt and Cinders as Wyatt drove into the homestead at Taylor's View. After a morning signing all the necessary documents with Barbara's lawyer, the homestead was unconditionally theirs in three weeks in a joint ownership agreement. Even the somewhat large mortgage was divided fifty-fifty with automatic deductions from each of their accounts. Wyatt had insisted on this as they had each contributed half the deposit. It was a stretch for Ellie but she now owned her original home from her former marriage to Jaxon and Wyatt assured her he would get a good price for the house when he sold it.

"Oh Wyatt," Ellie gasped as the sun shone down on them when they drove in. They climbed out, let Cinders have his usual sniffing trip and Ellie clung onto her sunhat as she stepped into his arms. "Look at that view. I feel I can just about each out and touch the city."

"Don't try," Wyatt replied with a laugh. 'There's a cliff beyond the edge of our property. Shall we go inside? Barbara told me to keep the key I had when I was her agent. She also said she didn't mind if we brought stuff in even before it becomes legally ours."

"A splendid old lady and I was impressed with her daughter, too. "

"Yes Alice actually thanked me for persuading her mother to sell their homestead. Barbara's new villa at the village in Auckland will be ready when she goes north."

When they walked inside, Ellie felt a buzz of excitement as Wyatt described some of the renovations he was thinking about.

"Pity about those new windows at the old place," he said as they stepped out onto the back veranda. "They would have fitted in here perfectly."

Ellie laughed. "A whole homestead gone and you commiserate about two sets of windows?"

"We'll need to buy some beef cattle to graze our farm. They're better than sheep for they don't take so much looking after. In spring we can buy in calves that we keep until they become yearlings then sell them off to make a huge profit."

" What's a yearling?" Ellie asked.

"A young cow or steer between one and two years old."

"Interesting. So we can both give up our jobs and become farmers?"

Wyatt laughed. "Doubt it. Alternatively we could lease the land out and let somebody else do the same thing." He glanced down at her. "So you'll shift in with me?"

Ellie nodded. "I thought that was a foregone conclusion? I was talking about it with Annette. She wants to take over the lease of my apartment when I shift out. Her new one is held up yet again and her new rent will be almost doubled, too."

"I heard that there is quite a protest by the present tenants there. The owners of your apartment are just a couple and not an overseas conglomerate. My company handles all their rentals so it won't be hard to just switch the tenancy to Annette."

"That's great." Ellie glanced around. "Where's Cinders?"

"Behind you," Wyatt chuckled. "If you had stepped back you would have tripped over him."

"Hi Cinders," Ellie said as she squatted down to pat him. "How do you like our new home?"

JAXON WAS IN THE EXERCISE yard within the remand prison with twenty or so fellow remand prisoners who were deemed to be low risk. They were kept away from more violent remand prisoners. These were either gang members who again were separated between the different gangs or at the other end of the social scale, embezzlers or those charged with money laundering or importing illegal drugs.

Apart from the loss of pride at being there, he had coped quite well and had struck up a friendship with some of the other remand prisoners. He had suffered from the lack of access to alcohol but had found his appetite had improved and he had put on weight.

Two guards came up to him.

"The police are here to see you, Jaxon," one said. "Please come to the interview room."

Jaxon's hope rose. Perhaps his lawyer's request for bail had been granted or, with a little luck, charges may have been dropped altogether. After all, it was all circumstantial evidence against him.

"Good luck to you, Mate," the guy he had been talking to said.

"You too, Wiremu. I hope your court case goes well next week."

Wiremu shrugged. "Thanks Mate, whatever happens it will be better than just waiting in here."

Immediately upon walking into the interview room and seeing a two grim face senior uniformed police officers and a woman in plain clothes, probably a detective sitting behind a table, his hopes of something good happening plummeted.

The woman stood up. "Mr Jaxon Parkes, I am Detective Sergeant Layla Fraser. Concrete evidence has been found to link you to the fire at the Sigley Homestead as well as the Hillview Apartments in High Street, Hutt City. The original charges against you stand. However, in addition I arrest you for arson and murder and caution you that anything you..."

She continued with the usual caution but Jaxon had stopped listening. He stared at her in utter disbelief. The room began to spin and all he could hear was his heart racing seemingly between his ears. He clutched at the table in front of him but missed and collapsed to the floor.

LAYLA WAS UNSYMPATHETIC as she watched as a medic rushed in, bend down beside the unconscious Jaxon and felt for his pulse.

He looked up. "His heart is racing but he should awaken soon. We'll take him to the infirmary."

"Pity," she whispered. "He's a criminal who shows no remorse about his actions, what-so-ever."

"Just be careful with your comments, Layla," Inspector Caleb Stewart said. "I have been advised that his lawyer is going to claim police discrimination against him with the aim of getting no circumstantial evidence allowed in his trial."

"So we get more concrete evidence and reliable witnesses."

"Keep working on it, Layla," the inspector said. "I am pulling you off that latest murder that is really quite straight forward so you can devote more time on proving these latest charges. Will that help?"

"It certainly will, Sir," Layla replied grimly. "That screw top was just one of the items the forensic team is looking at."

CHAPTER 19

At school, they were well into the last term of the year. November was one of busiest times on the school calendar with parent interviews, final yearly reports of children's progress and preparation of the traditional Christmas class trips and parties. Also, teachers had peer evaluations as well as Ellie's own evaluations of syndicate and classroom progress.

She was tired but a happy with fewer problems from parents or administrators than in the previous year.

"Here's my assessment of everything I've been doing as your deputy," Janice said in one of their reporting back sessions that Ellie had with all her senior staff. "I must say that I am doing far more now than I used to do under your predecessor but am enjoying it more." She grinned. "Your so called hands-on approach that I opposed when you brought it in has helped us all, you know."

Ellie nodded. "I realise I had to pull rank several times and actually persuaded Maurine that it might be her time to retire. She's sixty-six, you know."

"And has been here for twenty odd years. Her husband died the year before you arrived and I think school is all she had."

"Did he?" Ellie replied. "I didn't know. Perhaps I was too harsh on her."

"No. That gentle nudge you made was what she needed. Her daughter has actually persuaded her to buy into a retirement village in

Auckland where they live. I think she is looking forward to it and being close to grandkids."

They continued on their conversation for another twenty minutes before Janice packed up and glanced at her. "You look tired, Ellie. Are you looking after yourself?"

"Me?" Ellie replied. "I'm like us all in November, I guess. Wyatt actually suggested that I visit my doctor for a bit of a check up."

"And you're doing it."

Ellie grinned and nodded. "Tomorrow morning, actually. I should have told you I've an early appointment but won't be in until about ten. Okay?"

DOCTOR DALYA XIANG was of Chinese descent and had become Ellie's doctor at the clinic three years earlier. She was pleasant and very approachable and in many ways was like the modern New Zealand teachers compared with those of her profession from the earlier generation.

"I haven't seen you since that escapade in the ranges. I hope you are looking after yourself and not working too hard. I've heard that being a school principal is one of the most stressful occupations there is," Dalya began

Ellie grinned. "About equal to being a family doctor."

Dalya smiled. "Possibly but how can I help you today?"

"Wyatt, that's my partner has suggested I come for a routine check up."

"And so you should. So let's start with your blood pressure..."

The doctor did routine tests and after several minutes complimented Ellie on her overall health. She did though, frown and said there was one last test she should do. A urine test seemed routine enough so Ellie slipped through to the toilet and brought back a sample.

Mere moments late Dalya nodded as if the sample she tested seemed to confirm something that she had expected.

Ellie frowned. "Is there a problem?" she asked

"No. Perfectly natural." The doctor smiled at her. "You're pregnant, Ellie. Didn't you guess?"

"What!" Ellie responded. "But I thought I couldn't have children."

The doctor scrolled up the notes on her computer and studied an entry. "Remember a couple of years back I said there was no reason that you couldn't conceive and this has proved that I was right."

"But!" Ellie gasped.

"I believed then and still do, that it was your ex-husband who was infertile and not you. I noted that I mentioned it at that time."

Ellie's heart pounded. "He refused any tests and said he never wanted kids, anyway. I know I missed a period but I am always irregular. This has happened before and I just put it down to all the stress during in the year."

"I hope it's a pleasant surprise," Dalya replied. "I think you've been having that so-called morning sickness. My estimate is that you're about a month into your first semester. My suggestion is that we get you a mid-wife. We have a couple of excellent ones that we refer our mothers-to-be to."

"Oh my God," Ellie responded. "That's wonderful. Mother-to-be! I've never been called that before."

"Congratulations," Dalya replied and looked as though she really meant it.

"SO HOW DID IT GO?" Wyatt who had been waiting with his new Land Cruiser that he had just picked up after deciding to pay the difference from the vehicle insurance payout and the cost of a new vehicle.

Ellie grinned. "So you like new things?" she said as she climbed aboard the shiny vehicle.

"Yeah sure do but why are you acting so mysteriously?"

"New car, new baby. Won't they fit in well together?"

Wyatt, who was about to start the Land Cruiser, turned and just stared.

"What?" he gasped.

"I've been pregnant for a month now. You're going to be a daddy in the new year. When one plays with fire, you know..."

"But!"

"That's what I said to Doctor Xiang."

'The one who said there was no reason you couldn't have children?"'

'That's her," Ellie replied.

Suddenly Wyatt reached across, seized her in a tight hug and plastered kisses on her lips.

"So it's lucky that we shifted into Taylor's View together, isn't it?" he said after they became disentangled.

"So you'd better get that spare bedroom restored," Ellie replied.

"What?"

"Oh stop muttering 'what' all the time. That's something else I haven't told you. My divorce is legal now. By the time our baby arrives my marriage to Jaxon would have been annulled." Ellie placed her finger on Wyatt's lips. "And if you say 'what' again, I'll scream."

"Glory be!" Wyatt replied and kissed her again.

ANOTHER FINAL HAPPENING that Ellie and her Board of Trustees had to attend to before the end of the school year was to make the new appointments of teachers for the following year. A junior teacher had resigned from her position and was leaving on an extended trip to United Kingdom and Diane the senior teacher who ran the parallel syndicate to Janice's one for half the year was retiring.

Due to their expanded roll numbers in the new year there was also one more basic teacher's position that had been advertised. It was the Board of Trustees that made these appointments but they relied on Ellie as principal to make most recommendations for the short listed candidates. These teachers would be invited to an interview that included Ellie, after which the strongest candidate would be offered the position.

This was straightforward except for the senior teacher's position to replace Diane. Ellie told Brian Fleming, the Board Of Trustees chairman that to avoid any conflict of interest she would withdraw from helping in the selection of a new senior teacher.

Brain who was in her office to discuss the appointments nodded. "I thought you might but it isn't really necessary, you know."

"Well I recommended that Kerenza Bardell should apply for the position. You know about the split up with Janice at the beginning of the year. She certainly proved her worth when she became under my direct care and also did well with Diane in the last two terms."

"So?"

"To be fair on the other candidates who applied for the position I should be seen as being fair to everyone so don't wish to be on the section committee for that vacancy."

"But everyone knows you will be scrupulously professional in making any selection."

Ellie shrugged. "Any outside candidate won't. I not only have to be fair but must be seen to be fair by strangers who do not know me."

Brian shrugged. "Fair enough but we need a staff representative on the appointments committee."

"How about Margaret? She teaches in the junior school and hasn't been involved in the changes we made in the senior school."

Margaret Fitzsimmons was the staff representative on the BOT.

"Okay," Brian said. "I know Margaret will be fair to everyone applying for the position."

In the next week, Kerenza was short listed and attended an interview that included three other short-listed a candidates, all outsiders from the city and other parts of the country. It was held in the school staffroom on the Tuesday morning. Afterwards the selection committee would meet and make that important final selection.

Ellie was shown the results on Wednesday and the candidates informed by email the same evening.

Just before ten that evening her iPhone rang.

"I got the senior teacher's position," Kerenza almost screamed from the iPhone. "And don't tell me you had nothing to do with it."

"I had nothing to do with it, Kerenza. I told you that but congratulations. You deserve it."

"Oh Ellie, can I shout you and Wyatt a meal to celebrate?"

Ellie grinned at Wyatt who was listening. "Of course. We'll love to come."

After chatting for several minutes Kerenza clicked off.

Wyatt grimaced at Ellie. "So next year, you will have two parallel Year 3 to 6 syndicates, the oh so formal Janice running one and the oh so informal Kerenza running the other. Won't sparks fly?"

"I doubt it. Janice has mellowed and Kerenza has changed too. Otherwise she wouldn't have won the position."

'True," Wyatt replied. "Sometimes I'm glad I'm just a guy selling houses for a living."

Ellie stepped over and l kissed him. "You're not just a guy selling houses, Wyatt. You're a successful business man that I am proud of."

IN NEW ZEALAND THE summer school holidays extended from mid-December through until the beginning of February. Ellie enjoyed the time away from the school and apart from one trip back to Greystone Beach they chose to remain at home during the holidays. The site of the old homestead had been bulldozed off with only a couple of smaller buildings, including a pump shed remaining. Wyatt sold the land to the owners of South Pacific View Station at a good price that reflected the current trends.

Ellie's pregnancy progressed well with no problems except that she was beginning to show her condition. Without exception, everyone at work were thrilled and the Board Of Trustees recommended that she take the first term off as maternity leave. This right was well used by the teaching profession with around eighty-five percent of New Zealand teachers being female and most of them were within the child bearing ages. This would take her to the beginning of May and probably after Jaxon's trial that was tentatively set to begin in early April in the new year.

Taylor's View Homestead, the name they had decided to keep, looked no different from the outside. Perhaps there not as many flowers in the garden compared with Barbara's time but the Wyatt kept the gardens tidy and hedges trimmed. He almost clucked around Ellie and wouldn't let her do any heavy gardening work.

"I' pregnant not incapacitated," she said when he stopped her trying to start the lawnmower one hot morning. "Even though I'm on holiday, you've got several clients to see this morning and that suburban block of shops is being auctioned after lunch."

"The auctioneer doesn't need me. Leave the lawns and I'll come home this afternoon and mow them."

"Yes Sir," Ellie replied and gave a mock salute. "When are the calves we bought arriving?"

"Tomorrow. I picked them up at the last sale before Christmas. It's late January before they have another local one." He grinned. "They're all steers and were half the price of the heifers."

"And next year when we sell them?"

"They're mainly bought to raise for meat so the price doesn't vary a lot."

"You hope," Ellie said. She turned to Cinders who was never far away. "Well, with no lawn to mow what say take a walk around the farm?"

Cinders looked up and wagged his tail.

"And wear a sunhat." Wyatt ordered.

"Nag, nag, nag!" Ellie muttered as, followed by Cinders, she walked away. She was happy though, perhaps more so than any time in her life. Everything was slipping into place and even Jaxon's impending trial was a black cloud that she ignored.

"And no chasing rabbits," she warned Cinders. "You wouldn't know what to do if you caught one, anyway."

Cinders gave a woof and totally ignoring her, dashed off across the paddock in search of prey.

CHAPTER 20

Jaxon Parkes' trial was in the third day of an estimated week allocated for it. He had been charged with the murder of the two people at Hillview Apartments, attempted murder of his estranged wife, Ellie Parkes, arson of two buildings, that of Hillview Apartments in High Street, Hutt City and South Pacific View Homestead at the locality of Greystone Beach and five other lesser charges.

The Crown Prosecutor's case was almost complete with one final witness about to take the stand. This was Ellie who reluctantly agreed to appear after first refusing to take any part.

The clerk stood up. "The Crown calls Mrs Ellie Parkes to the witness box," he called out in a formal voice.

"Will you be okay?" Wyatt said to Ellie in the Witness Waiting Room when she was approached by an usher.

"I'm fine, Wyatt." she replied.

Even though dressed in a modest blue smock it was obvious that she was in the last stages of her pregnancy with actually only a couple of weeks to go before the anticipated birth of their baby boy. She entered the courtroom through a side door and had to walk a few metres to the witness box that did really look like a box with an open back where a witness could walk in. The surrounding box-like sides and front were a little over hip high and there was a small shelf on the inside that contained only a microphone. There was a comfortable chair like a kitchen one to sit on.

"You can sit down until you are called upon to speak," the usher said. "If you find it difficult to stand for a long period you can ask to sit," He looked embarrassed. "Due to your, err, condition, this will be allowed."

"Thank you," Ellie said and sat down. More or less diagonally across from her and further back in the room she saw Jaxon. He was dressed in a business suit, something he never wore but did look slimmer than she remembered. His expression though looked the same; that defiant expression with a pout and downcast eyes turned away from her.

She chose to make an affirmation rather than a religious oath and turned slightly towards the judge as she repeated words asked of her. Afterwards she sat down again and waited.

"I call upon Mrs Ellie Parkes," the Crown Prosecutor announced.

Ellie stood up and turned slightly to face to her left. In doing so her profile and rotund pregnancy was in full view of the court members.

She heard that oh so familiar scream from across the court and turned.

"You wore," Jaxon screamed. "You stupid cow! For years we wanted to have a child and you slept around and... " Words that she couldn't comprehend followed but ended with, "I'll show you nobody defies me."

She turned and gasped as Jaxon leaped over the desk he stood behind and shaking in fury, charged towards her. His fists were held up like that of a boxer.

It all happened within seconds and even in the sanctuary of the courtroom she was terrified. She froze and grasped the tiny shelf before her. Emotions surged and without warning tears streamed down her face as brutal memories interrupted the actual scene before her.

In a haze before her, she could see that Jaxon was already half way across the space between them. Everything that was a blur suddenly became focused.

She saw the Crown Prosecutor step out but instead of trying to grab the enraged Jaxon, he stuck out his foot and tripped him up. Jaxon went sprawling across the floor and was seized by two court attendants.

He was screaming and fighting but was held down by security guards who had arrived.

A gentle hand touched Ellie. "Just sit down Ellie." Kind words from the usher who had just escorted her in spoke. "He cannot reach you."

There was no pain but a minor popping sensation and a trickle of unstoppable fluid flowed down her legs. This increased in volume and Ellie stared down at her wet smock and a puddle of water beneath the pushed back chair.

She glanced up and caught the lady judge's eyes.

"I'm sorry, My Lady. I think my water has broken."

MEANWHILE JAXON HAD begun to fight and scream incoherently. He was handcuffed, dragged to his feet and held firmly by a guard.

"Remove the defendant from the courtroom," the judge stated in an icy voice and turned to Ellie. "The court apologises unconditionally to you, Mrs Parkes. Given the circumstances you are excused from being a witness but may later make a victim statement that will be read to the jury. Both the prosecuting and defence counsel will meet in my chambers forthwith. Meanwhile the morning session is cancelled but the case will convene at the usual time this afternoon. "

Everyone in the courtroom stood as she turned and left the chambers. A stunned silence continued and Jaxon who was now also silent was literally dragged out.

Wyatt appeared and ignoring everyone, escorted her out of the courtroom and into a small anti-room that made Ellie think of a doctor's surgery.

"Oh Wyatt, I'm so so sorry," she sobbed as he helped her onto a stretcher in the room.

"For what?" Wyatt replied. "Showing his true nature this will be his undoing."

Suddenly, she felt a spasm of pain as a contraction raked though her body and clutched into him

FIVE HOURS LATER, THREE kilogram Marvin Richard Sigley arrived in the Hutt Hospital Maternity Ward two weeks early. The name Marvin that both Ellie and Wyatt chose meant a hill by the sea and Richard was Ellie's father's name. Apart from this unexpected arrival, Ellie's midwife declared that the baby was in perfect condition.

News spread like wild fire and by mid-morning a steady steam of flowers, cards and gifts filled her alcove. Most of the staff from school arrived as did Annette, Scarlett and Narla, with them all bearing flowers and gifts for Marvin and herself.

Wyatt arrived for the third time with a rubber bone and grapes in his hand. "They wouldn't let Cinders in so he sent his favourite bone for you to munch on," he said.

"I hope he hasn't slobbered all over it," Ellie said in a deadpan voice. "And more grapes! Have you got shares in the local vineyard?"

THE FOLLOWING MORNING, Ellie insisted on sitting in an armchair in her alcove to make her statement. Though it was less formal than being in the actual trial, the judge, Crown Prosecutor and defence lawyer asked her questions. Also she was allowed to tell about everything in her own words. Wyatt was there as a support person but had to stay quiet even though at times he looked as if he wanted to add things to her statement.

Even the defence lawyer was considerate and made no cutting cross-examination remarks that he had made to Annette and other witnesses at the trial itself.

"I have just one last question," he said. "Jaxon stated in the trial yesterday afternoon that you knew Wyatt and had along term affair with him before you met on the beach. However earlier in the trial Wyatt insisted that you were strangers when he rescued you out of the surf during that winter storm at Greystone Beach. Who was correct?"

"Wyatt told the truth and Jaxon lied. I had no earlier affair with Wyatt nor with anyone else to that date," Ellie whispered. "Jaxon was the one who had numerous affairs when we were together."

"When your statement is read before the court tomorrow, I'm sure the jury will know who to believe," the judge added. She stood, shook Ellie's hand and departed.

"This is off the record but this one case I don't mind losing," the defence lawyer said after the judge had gone. "Our case really just fell apart after his outburst. I could tell by the expressions on the jurors' faces when the trial recommenced."

AFTER DELIBERATING for four hours the jury filed back into courtroom and told the judge they had reached their verdicts. A slip of paper was handed to the registrar who handed it onto the judge. She read it with no emotion showing, glanced at the head juror and asked the usual questions before coming to the verdicts themselves.

"To the two charges of murder of Mrs Joanne Keech and Mr Thomas Keech how to you find the defendant?" she asked.

"Not guilty to murder but guilty to the lesser charge of manslaughter," the foreperson of the jury replied.

"To the charge of attempted murder of Mrs Ellie Parkes, his legal wife at that time?"

"Guilty, Your Honour..."

And so it continued. Jaxon was found guilty to both arson charges and every other charge on the list,

The judged turned to face Jaxon. "You have been found guilty to manslaughter, attempted murder, two counts of arson and ..." She listed every charge before continuing. "You will be held in custody until the twentieth of next month when your sentences will be announced. However, you can expect a lengthy custodial term, Mr Parkes. Take the prisoner away."

Ellie who was in the public gallery holding Marvin in her arms glanced up at Wyatt who was standing beside her before switching her eyes to Jaxon. He appeared to be barely able to walk as he was escorted from the courtroom.

"So that's it?" she whispered, handed the baby to Wyatt to hold and with her head held high left the courtroom.

THEY VISITED A NEARBY coffee bar where Ellie took back Marvin who had dropped asleep. They had another hour before the baby's next feeding time. They chatted about events and were about to leave when a police sergeant approached them.

"Mrs Ellen Parkes?" he asked.

Ellie frowned. "I am, Sergeant. "

"Could you please accompany me back to the court house for a few moments when you have finished your coffee?

"Why?"

He looked empathetic rather than authoritative. "Everything will be explained."

"Only if my partner and baby can come, too," Ellie responded.

"Of course they can."

She glanced at Wyatt who gave a slight shrug. They followed the sergeant the fifty or so metres back to a courthouse side door signposted as being only for court staff and into a common room.

There the judge and both main lawyers from the trial sat in a circle of armchairs together with a stranger.

They were greeted by their forenames and asked to sit. They did and the stranger introduced himself. "I am Doctor Norman McAllen, today's on-call court physician. An incident has happened that you need to be informed about. Can I be blunt?"

"Please just tell me what's wrong," Ellie replied.

"Jaxon never made it out of the court house. After leaving the courtroom he collapsed and in spit of efforts of those around, died from a probable massive heart attack."

Ellie just stared at him. Strangely, she felt nothing and an emptiness that filled her body.

"I know Jaxon had a heart flutter but he refused to visit a doctor about it," she finally said. "There was nothing sinister, I hope."

The doctor shook his head. "As with all unexpected deaths, the body will be referred to a coroner but in my opinion his death was entirely from natural causes and brought about by shock at the trial's outcome." He coughed. "It is a formality, I know but sometime today could you officially identify the body?"

"Can I do it now?"

"There is no urgency."

"I wish to do it now?" Ellie found herself shaking. She handed Marvin back to Wyatt and stood up. "Please," she whispered.

She was led into the same medical room where she had been earlier and noticed a sheet-covered body on the bed. The doctor lifted the sheet from the face that she instantly recognised.

"It is Jaxon Parkes, my former husband," she said. "Is that all you need me for?"

"Yes, thank you," replied the doctor. "Your help has been appreciated."

HAVING A NEW BABY WAS hard work but Ellie coped well and had taken to the occasional daytime nap when Marvin was asleep. There were the usual rashes and so forth that little ones have but Wyatt was so helpful, it was almost embarrassing. It was now the beginning of the second term with the next step in her busy life.

Marvin was a chubby little fellow and fitted in well at the *Tiny Tots Academy,* a pre-school facility only a block away from school that took new infants to four-year-olds. She or Wyatt would drop him off at eight and on most days Wyatt would pick him up at four.

Cinders became the self appointed guardian of the baby. On the few occasions in town when she had to dash into a pharmacy or bank, Cinders would just sit beside the buggy. If anyone appeared threatening the dog would stand and growl slightly through his teeth. The large black Labrador took his duty seriously.

Back at school, Ellie found that everything during her time away had continued on well. As acting principal Janice had followed her methods but at times it was Kerenza who had dealt with parents complaints or with children needing discipline. Both though, told her they were glad she as back and they could return to their syndicate and other duties.

She was in her office on the second week back when Detective Layla Fraser called in.

"Hi Layla," Ellie said. "I guess you're as busy as usual."

Layla smiled and accepted a seat. "Like yourself. How do you cope with the school and baby?"

"Busy but satisfying."

"We just got the final report on Jaxon's death back from the coroner. It appears that he did indeed die from a massive heart attack. However, he had substantial amounts of illegal drugs in his system that contributed to his seizure and death. Without them he may have survived the attack. "

"But how did he get drugs in remand prison?"

"That's something I have been assigned to investigate. It's a never-ending battle. No sooner do we close one door and another opens. We have however, improved the systems and two guards who had been bribed by prisoners have been dismissed."

Ellie sighed. "I doubt if Jaxon would have lasted for long in prison anyway. The gang members would have picked on him."

"True," Layla replied. "They have their own moral and loyalty codes that would make him a targeted enemy." She stood up. "But I must away. Keep in touch and say hi to Wyatt from me."

"Sure will. Remember our PTA want you to come and speak at one of our monthly meetings."

"I'll be there," Layla replied. "The May meeting, I think it is."

She smiled and left the room.

THE LAWYER'S OFFICE that Ellie visited was quite familiar as it was the one her parents as well as herself had used when she was younger. She glanced around the somewhat dated waiting room and even remembered one rural painting that she had admired when visiting on a few occasions while waiting for her father.

Her parents' lawyer had long gone but the man that greeted her looked vaguely familiar.

"I'm Peter Giles but call me Pete. We have met," he said after they shook hands. He opened a document on his desk and turned it around for her to see.

She skipped the heading but noticed her own and Jaxon's signature at the bottom of the page. "So what is it?" she asked

"Your joint life insurance that you both signed not long after your marriage. I was the witness to the document." He sort of nodded. "We had to check a couple of items that had to be confirmed before the insurance company would honour it."

"And they were?"

"The first was that you were still Jaxon Parkes' legal wife at the time of his death. Is that true?"

"I guess so. We were legally separated but my divorce had still to come through."

"That is what we checked on and found to be correct as it does affect the payout," Pete said. "The other major condition was held up until the coroner's report on his death was released. It confirmed that he died of natural causes and did not commit suicide. If he had, this would have invalidated the claim."

"I see. So it is all legal now?"

"Yes. You are entitled to six hundred thousand dollars that can be paid into a bank account of your choosing."

Ellie gasped.

"It would have been over a million if he had died by accident," Pete continued.

Ellie frowned. "And if I had died first?" she asked.

"Jaxon Parkes would have received the payout. Insurance companies don't encourage these policies now but of course they are obliged to honour existing ones."

"And if I had died in a fire?" Ellie gasped.

"That would have been an accidental death."

"The bastard! It all ties in," Ellie whispered to herself and told Pete briefly about the homestead and Annette's apartment fires. "In the court case he was proved guilty of arson for both fires."

"A nasty little man." Pete muttered before he broke into a smile. "If you sign this document and give me a bank account number we can transfer the payout into your account."

THOUGH HER LUNCH BREAK had already been extended, Ellie drove to Wyatt's office and found him there.

He looked up and frowned. "Ellie," he gasped. "What's wrong and why aren't you at school?"

"Been to our old lawyer," she replied and slapped the policy on his desk. "Our joint life insurance. Jaxon and me had it made up not long after we were married. It's all valid and you know that second mortgage we need after that bridging finance to pay for Taylor's View?"

"Of course I do. I was going to tell you I couldn't get the interest rate lowered.'

"We don't need it, Wyatt. Six hundred thousand will more than cover everything."

"What?" Wyatt gasped.

"The insurance payout!"

Wyatt stood, walked around his desk and embraced her in a massive hug. They kissed and he grinned. "So you aren't just a pretty face after all."

"Watch it!" Ellie retorted. "I might begin to think you're marrying me for my money."

ALONG WITH THIS UNEXPECTED insurance payout, Ellie was listed as Jaxon's next of kin as he had not bothered to change it after she left him. This included their old home, his vehicles and other personal belongings.

Wyatt had already bought in painters to upgrade the interior of the house as it had become rundown since she had shifted out. They were also having new carpet and curtains put in. Their plan was to place it on the market as it was in a popular part of town and with the interior upgrade, Wyatt estimated that they would get more than these added costs once it was sold.

She kept some furniture, mainly the modern suite and bedroom that she had originally paid for but his clothing and so forth were donated to a local charity, as were a washing machine and other utilities in the house. They also decided to keep his camper van but decided to sell his car and motorbike as well as other items worth selling. His clothing and so forth were donated to a local charity, as were smaller items in the house.

"There's not much left of a human life," Ellie said to Wyatt as she stared around the now empty rooms.

"Empty homes always lack personality," Wyatt said. "That is why we have several sets of furniture to place in empty houses that we sell. It's amazing how much difference it makes when we are showing people through them."

"It wasn't always bad," she said wistfully as she thought back to the time she lived in the house.

"I know. I feel the same about my marriage to Jennifer."

Ellie nodded. "Yeah but at least she didn't try to bump you off to claim the life insurance money."

THE END

Don't miss out!

Visit the website below and you can sign up to receive emails whenever Ross Richdale publishes a new book. There's no charge and no obligation.

https://books2read.com/r/B-A-QEXC-TUNWB

BOOKS 2 READ

Connecting independent readers to independent writers.

Also by Ross Richdale

Emerald Eyes Trilogy
Emerald Eyes Destiny
Emerald Eyes Mist
Emerald Eyes Pyramid

Our Ancient Ancestors
When the Longships Came
The Druid's Daughter
Meztli - Sacrificial Maiden
Kyla's Fate

Our Romantic Thrillers
Blemished Jewel
Jana Adrift
Broken Silence
Eagle's Claw Lake
Snow Bond
Blossoms in the Wind

Terra Novels

The Truth About Terra

Terra Incognita

Wisps Trilogy

Wisps of Cloud

Wisps of Snow

Wisps of Wisdom

Standalone

Solar Search

Acid Air

Embrace the Fog

Cosmos Quest

Azure Sea Gold

Alien Hybrid

Crystal Souls

Countess In Exile

Anu Factor

Into the Wormhole

Time Portal

Like Twigs in a Storm

Omega Seed

Catalyst

Long Valley Road

Armlet

Claire

Liberty & Opportunity

Transmigration
Shadows Behind
Wind Across the Playground
Arising Magic
Generation 7
The Other Mrs Hayes
Stretched Horizons
Behind the Fire
Hatchlings
Affinity & Trust
Watershed Law
Astrid's Coast
Mind Split
Infinity Drive Missions
Turbulence

Watch for more at www.richdale.co.nz.

About the Author

After a career as a teacher and principal of mainly small rural schools, Ross Richdale lives in the small university city of Palmerston North in the North Island of New Zealand where he writes contemporary novels and science fiction. He is married with three adult children and six grandchildren.

His interest in current events and international incidents serve as a backdrop for many of his novels. Ordinary people rather than the super rich super powerful or violent, are the main characters in his stories. His plots also reflect his interest in the rural lifestyle as well as the cross section of personalities encountered during his years as a teacher.

Read more at www.richdale.co.nz.

www.ingramcontent.com/pod-product-compliance
Ingram Content Group UK Ltd.
Pitfield, Milton Keynes, MK11 3LW, UK
UKHW041827200726
13854UKWH00002BA/629